Hide and Shriek

Randy knows the twelve-year-olds of Shadyside play a big game of hide-and-seek in the woods every June. Sounds like fun, she thinks. Until she finds out who's "it." A ghost named Pete who wants to tag Randy and take over her body forever.

Spell of the
Screaming Jokers

Brittany and her friends agree to play cards with Max, a sick kid from their class. But the jokers in Max's magic deck are alive! And they're evil!

Field of Screams

Buddy always wanted to play on the best baseball team in Shadyside. But he never dreamed he'd be sent to the past to do it—or that his very life would depend on winning!

Also from R.L. Stine

The Beast®
The Beast® 2

R.L. Stine's Ghosts of Fear Street

Available from MINSTREL Books

R·L·STINE'S
GHOSTS OF FEAR STREET®

CREEPY COLLECTION #3:
THE SCREAM TEAM

A Parachute Book

A MINSTREL® BOOK

Published by POCKET BOOKS
New York   London   Toronto   Sydney   Tokyo   Singapore

These titles were previously published individually.

A Minstrel Paperback published by
POCKET BOOKS, a division of Simon & Schuster Inc.
1230 Avenue of the Americas, New York, NY 10020

Hide and Shriek copyright © 1995 by Parachute Press, Inc.
Spell of the Screaming Jokers copyright © 1997 by Parachute Press, Inc.
Field of Screams copyright © 1997 by Parachute Press, Inc.

HIDE AND SHRIEK WRITTEN BY EMILY JAMES
SPELL OF THE SCREAMING JOKERS WRITTEN BY KATHY HALL
FIELD OF SCREAMS WRITTEN BY P. MacFEARSON

ISBN: 0-671-02294-6

First Minstrel Books paperback printing June 1998

10 9 8 7 6 5 4 3 2

FEAR STREET is a registered trademark of Parachute Press, Inc.

A MINSTREL BOOK and colophon are registered trademarks of Simon & Schuster Inc.

Cover art by John Youssi

Printed in the U.S.A.

GHOSTS of FEAR STREET®

HIDE AND SHRIEK

HIDE AND SHRIEK

"Randy! Randy!" My little sister, Baby, wiggled into my room. "Mom says she's going to kill you."

She giggled. She loves to see me get into trouble. Mostly because she's always in trouble herself.

I ignored Baby and yelled down the stairs at my mother. "Stop bugging me, Mom! I'm coming!"

"You're going to be late!" Mom yelled back.

"I know! I can't help it!"

It was my first day at Shadyside Middle School. I didn't want to be late. But I didn't want to show up looking like a dork, either. I'd tried on everything in my closet. Nothing looked right. All my clothes looked babyish on me, which is the last thing I need.

I'm twelve, but people always think I'm younger.

I don't see it, myself. I think I have a very mature face. I am small and wiry. But I'm not *that* small. I wasn't even the smallest girl in the class at my old school.

Some people are so stupid. They don't look at the facts.

I stared at myself in the mirror, tugging at the waist of my jeans. What did the kids in Shadyside wear, anyway? I had no clue. I'd only lived here for two days.

My family—me, Mom, Dad, and my insane little sister—just moved to Shadyside from Maine. We live on Fear Street.

It's a weird name for a street, I think. Fear Street. Not exactly cheery.

Even Shadysiders seem to think the street name is weird. The day we moved in, I went to the post office with Mom, and the clerk gave us a funny look when Mom mentioned our address.

The clerk raised her eyebrows and said, "Fear Street, hmm?"

I thought the clerk was pretty weird herself. She stared at me really hard and then asked how old I was.

"Twelve," I told her.

"Then you might be the one," she commented.

My mom and I exchanged confused glances.

"The one what?" I couldn't resist asking.

"You'll find out soon enough—if you aren't careful," she answered mysteriously. "June tenth is right around the corner. You've moved to town at the perfect time."

Yeah, right, I thought. It's great starting a new school at the end of the year. I had to finish the last month of sixth grade in a new school with a bunch of kids I didn't know.

And who didn't know me. And who'll take one look at me today, I thought, and decide right then and there if I'm cool or not.

I yanked off my jeans and tried on my gray jumper again. I wasn't sure it looked good with my brown hair. Mom stormed in.

"Randy, if you try on another stitch of clothing I'll scream. You're wearing that jumper, and that's final."

"Tell her, Mom," Baby said.

I made a face at Baby. She made one back at me.

"Girls!" Mom snapped.

Mom could be tough when she wanted to be. The jumper would have to do. I grabbed my backpack and raced out of the house.

Baby screeched after me, "You're going to be late! You're going to be late! Ha ha ha ha ha!"

Anybody want to adopt a seven-year-old girl?

3

I hurried down Fear Street and around the corner to Park Drive. When I got to Hawthorne, I started running.

Shadyside Middle School loomed ahead. The front doors were closed, and the school yard stood empty. I was definitely late.

Something about the sight of that empty school yard made my stomach flip over. Nervous, I guess. I ran up the steps and tugged on the door.

Locked!

I panicked. Locked out on my first day! Please don't let this be true.

I yanked on the door again. It didn't budge.

I almost burst into tears. What was I going to do?

I told myself to calm down. It can't be locked, I said to myself. They wouldn't lock all the kids inside the school, right? No, they wouldn't.

It helps to think things through like that. Sometimes I get kind of panicky, you know. Carried away by my imagination.

But I also have a sensible side. I can look at the facts. It helps keep my imagination from taking over.

I gave the door one last pull—and this time it flew open. My sensible side was right, I thought. As usual. The door sticks. No reason to get upset.

My footsteps echoed as I stepped into a long,

4

empty hallway. I shifted my backpack and nervously twirled my hair around a finger. I was supposed to report to the principal's office. But I had no idea where it was.

I passed row after row of classroom doors, all closed. Through the doors I heard teachers' voices and the shuffling of chairs. It made the silence of the hallway seem lonelier.

I hope I won't get into trouble for being late, I thought nervously. They wouldn't punish a kid on her first day, would they?

I passed a big bulletin board stuck to one wall. It was covered with announcements and end-of-the-year awards. In one corner someone had tacked a large calendar. It showed the months of May and June, with all the dates x-ed out up to that day, May twenty-second. One date had been circled in red felt-tip—Saturday, June tenth.

I wondered if there was a big game that day. Something about the tenth of June felt familiar. I'd heard something about it somewhere, I knew. The creepy woman in the post office, I remembered. She'd mentioned that date.

Then I noticed a scrawl at the top of the calendar: 18 MORE DAYS UNTIL PETE'S BIRTHDAY. The number was removable so it could be changed as time passed.

Wow, I thought. I wonder who Pete is. He must be pretty popular if the whole school is looking forward to his birthday.

I tore my eyes away from the bulletin board and turned a corner.

"Oh!" I gasped, stopping short. My feet slipped a little on the shiny floor.

A boy staggered toward me. But not a normal boy.

He stumbled forward, clutching his head. His face looked odd—greenish. He must be sick, I thought.

"What's the matter?" I asked. "What happened?"

He moaned in pain. "Help," he croaked. He reached out with bloody hands. Deep red blood oozed from a hideous gash in his head.

I screamed as the boy lurched toward me.

2

"**H**elp!" I cried.

I tried to run, but my feet felt glued to the floor.

The boy fell forward, his hands sticky with blood. I dodged him.

He slumped over, groaning. "My head . . . the pain . . ."

Feeling a little queasy, I bent over the boy. "Are—are you all right?" I asked.

What a stupid question. Blood trickled down his face. Anybody could see he wasn't all right.

The boy groaned louder. A teacher opened her door and stuck her head into the hallway.

"What's all the noise out here?" she demanded.

The bleeding boy suddenly straightened up. "Sorry, Ms. Munson," he said.

He hurried away, looking strangely healthy.

Ms. Munson stared at me. "You—where are you supposed to be?"

"I—I'm new," I stammered. "Where's the principal's office?"

The expression on her face softened a little. "Down this hall and to the right. Welcome to Shadyside!" She shut the door.

I started for the office. What happened to the bleeding boy? I wondered.

I heard a rustling noise, and a tall girl turned the corner and swished toward me. The girl wore a long green dress with a hoop skirt. Her brown hair was tucked under a white lace bonnet.

What a weird school, I thought.

The girl stopped. "Did you see a boy go by?" she asked me. "With blood coming out of his head?"

I nodded. "What happened to him?"

The girl laughed. "Nothing happened to him. It's a costume. We're in the school play, and Lucas plays a guy who gets killed."

"Oh," I said, relieved.

"We have dress rehearsal this morning," the girl said. "I've got to run." She paused. "Are you new? I've never seen you before."

I smiled. "I'm Randy Clay. This is my first day."

"Really?" the girl said. "So you're new. You're *really* new."

8

"Yes," I answered, confused. "I'm new." What was the big deal?

"Wow, I've got go," the girl said. "I'm late. Nice meeting you, Randy. My name's Sara Lewis. Hope I'll see you later. Bye!"

She ran down the hall, her skirts floating behind her.

I trudged toward the principal's office, shaking my head. What's going on? I wondered. Why is everybody so strange?

I stood outside the door of my sixth-grade class and took a deep breath. I was about to meet the kids who would be my friends from now on—if they liked me. And if I liked them.

I pulled open the door and stepped inside. The teacher, a small young woman with short dark hair, turned away from the blackboard. She smiled at me.

"Miranda Clay?" the teacher asked.

I nodded. "Everybody calls me Randy."

"I'm Ms. Hartman. Welcome. Why don't you take that empty seat in the third row?"

As I started for the empty seat, a buzz arose in the room. The kids stared at me and whispered to one another.

I tried to tell myself not to feel weird about it. They're just wondering who I am, I thought.

I sat next to a pretty girl with wavy blond hair. The girl stared at me, wide-eyed.

"Hi," I said to her.

The girl's eyes grew wider. She turned away from me and whispered to the red-haired girl next to her.

What is it? I wondered. Why are they whispering?

Maybe they're not whispering about me, I thought. I'm probably being too sensitive.

"Let's settle down," Ms. Hartman called.

The whispering gradually stopped.

Ms. Hartman said to me, "You'll be taking final exams during the last week of school. Have you ever taken a final exam before, Randy?"

I shook my head.

"Don't worry. No one else in the sixth grade has, either. Right now we're going over good ways to study and prepare. It's best not to save it until the last minute. . . ."

As the teacher spoke, I glanced around the room. The other kids didn't seem to be paying much attention to Ms. Hartman's study tips. Some of them were staring at me, or stealing glances at me out of the corners of their eyes. The two girls sitting next to me started whispering again.

At last a bell rang and we had recess. Most kids hurried outside. A couple of kids nodded to me and said hi.

"Do you play softball?" a girl asked me as we moved into the hall. She was big, with long dark hair in a braid down her back. A tall blond boy stood beside her.

"A little," I answered.

"We want to set up a coed softball team to play over the summer," the boy explained. He had an easy, friendly smile. I thought he was kind of cute.

"I'm Megan," the girl added. "And this is David."

"Hi," I said.

"I'll go to the gym and borrow a bat," David said. "Maybe we can hit a few during recess."

"Let's wait for him outside," Megan suggested. We stepped out into the bright sunlight.

A few feet ahead of me I noticed the blond girl—Laura—and her friend, Maggie. They turned around. Laura pointed at me.

I tried to ignore them, but it bothered me. What's their problem? I wondered.

"I'll be right back," I told Megan. I hurried inside and ran to the girls' bathroom.

Is something wrong with me? I thought. Have I got something stuck in my teeth? Is my hair sticking up?

I quickly checked myself out in the mirror.

I didn't have a huge pimple on my nose, or big

purple blotches on my cheeks, or a sign on my forehead saying, "Nut case." Nothing like that.

Nothing to explain the way the two girls were behaving.

I hurried back outside. Megan had gathered a bunch of kids together for softball. Sara, the girl I met in the hall, was one of them.

David returned with a bat and ball. "Why don't you play shortstop?" he suggested to me.

I always end up playing shortstop. Is there some rule that shortstops have to be short?

Anyway, I'm good at it from all the practice I get.

Laura and Maggie didn't play softball. They stood on the sidelines and watched.

The next day I saw Sara standing by the big bulletin board in the hall. She had a pen in her hand and was reading a notice on the board.

"Hi," I said. "What's up?"

She smiled. "Hi, Randy." She pointed at the notice she was reading. "I think I might sign up for this."

The notice said: VOLUNTEERS NEEDED TO MAKE PETE'S BIRTHDAY CAKE. SIGN YOUR NAME HERE.

That guy Pete again. I couldn't believe it. People were actually signing up to bake him a cake.

"What is this?" I asked Sara. "Who's Pete?"

"Don't you know?" Sara said. "Well—"

Suddenly I felt a presence behind me. Hot breath on my neck. I jumped and quickly turned around. Sara turned, too.

Laura stood there, reading over our shoulders. She'd crept up behind us so silently we didn't notice her until we felt her breath on our necks.

She glanced at the sign-up sheet. She raised an eyebrow. Then she whispered something to me. It sounded more like a hiss than a whisper.

Could Laura really have said such a mean thing to me?

It sounded as if she'd whispered, "You better watch out!"

3

I wandered through the crowded cafeteria a few days later, looking for Sara or Megan or David. All around me kids shouted, laughed, and joked, filling the room with noise. I relaxed a little.

For once this school feels normal, I thought. All week I've felt like an exhibit in a zoo. Everyone staring at the new girl.

Then I spotted Laura and Maggie. Maggie seemed to be Laura's sidekick or something. I'd never seen her even talking to anyone else.

It was pathetic.

Clutching my tray, I passed Laura and Maggie's table.

"Just wait," Laura murmured. "Just wait until the tenth."

My hands began to shake. This time I knew I hadn't imagined it. Was Laura threatening me?

What would happen on the tenth? I knew June tenth was Pete's birthday. But I still didn't know who Pete was.

I didn't know what to do. My hands shook so hard I was afraid I'd drop my tray in the middle of the lunchroom.

Then I saw someone waving to me from across the room. A skinny boy with curly black hair.

I didn't know who he was. I didn't care. I had to do something—anything.

I wanted to get away from Laura and Maggie as fast as possible. So I hurried toward the boy.

"Hi," he said. "Want to sit with me?"

"Sure," I replied. I still didn't know who the boy was, but he seemed to know me.

"I guess I scared you the other day," the boy said. "Sorry about that. It's like my costume takes over my personality."

I stared at him. What was he talking about?

"By the way," he went on, picking up his sandwich, "my name's Lucas."

Lucas? I thought. It sounded familiar. Oh, yes. Lucas! The boy with the bloody head!

"I'm Randy," I told him. "I didn't recognize you at first. I mean, without blood dripping down your face."

Lucas laughed. "Are you coming to see the play?" he asked me. "It's during the last week of school."

"Sure," I said. "What's it about?"

"It's a Sherlock Holmes mystery," Lucas answered. "The guy who plays Sherlock keeps messing up his lines. You know David Slater?"

"Yeah. He's in my class."

"He's the star of the play," Lucas said. "But he's terrible! I don't know why they picked him."

I opened my brown paper lunch bag and pulled out an apple. I like to eat my dessert first.

"That's too bad," I said between bites. I glanced across the room and caught Laura and Maggie watching me. They quickly turned their heads away.

"So where do you live?" Lucas asked.

"On Fear Street," I replied.

"Really? I live on Fear Street, too. Don't listen to the stories people tell about it. I've lived there all my life, and nothing bad has ever happened to me."

Stories? "What stories?" I asked.

Lucas shrugged. "People tell these crazy stories about Fear Street. Probably because of the name."

"It *is* a creepy name for a street," I admitted.

"You know that cemetery down the road?" Lucas said. "Some kids say it's haunted. My next-door neighbor told me he was riding his bike past there just before dark. He said a tall woman suddenly appeared and blocked his path. But he didn't have time to stop. He slammed on the brakes, but it was too late."

"What happened? Was she hurt?"

"That's the weird part," Lucas told me. "He *says*—if you believe him—that his bike went right through her. As if she were made of air."

"Wow! Was she a ghost?"

Lucas rolled his eyes. "Who knows? I think he was just trying to scare me. *I've* never seen any ghosts around there, myself."

I unwrapped my turkey sandwich but didn't bite into it.

I'm sure Lucas is right, I thought. People just like to tell scary stories.

But I couldn't help feeling uncomfortable. The name Fear Street had to come from something bad that had happened there. Didn't it?

I tilted my head back to catch the sunlight on my face. It felt good to be outside after a long day cooped up in school.

I walked home alone down Hawthorne Drive. My backpack, filled with all my new schoolbooks, hung heavily from my shoulders.

I'll use these books for a month, and then school's over, I thought. It's kind of stupid.

Deep, thick woods stretched out on my right, all

the way to Fear Street, where I lived. I could cut through the woods, I thought. It's probably the quickest way home.

I stepped off the sidewalk and into the woods. Darkness and quiet seemed to fall upon me like a blanket. The warm sunlight vanished.

I suddenly felt chilly. The hair rose on my arms. I rubbed them, shivering.

It's so quiet in here, I thought, glancing around at the tall trees and thick shrubs. No chirps or peeps or animal screeches. Why aren't there any birds or squirrels?

I found a little dirt path that seemed to take me in the right direction. I trudged along the path. The only sound was the crunch of twigs and leaves under my feet.

Crunch, crunch, crunch, crunch.

I walked for ten minutes before the woods began to thin.

I must be getting near the street again, I thought with relief. But I didn't hear the sounds of cars or people.

I came to a large clearing. Slabs of stone rose out of the ground.

Gravestones.

It's a cemetery, I realized.

I felt cold again.

Don't get scared, I scolded myself. The street is

on the other side of the cemetery, just beyond the woods. You're almost home.

No big deal, I thought. So you're walking through a cemetery. So what?

Think of the facts. After all, they're only dead people. Dead people can't hurt you. Because they're dead! Right?

I hurried past crumbling stone markers without stopping to read the names on them. I should be almost to my street, I thought.

Still the only sound I heard was the crackle of twigs under my feet. *Crunch, crunch, crunch, crunch.*

But then I thought I heard another sound. A sound I didn't want to hear.

I froze, listening. I scanned the cemetery and the woods beyond. I didn't see anyone. Nothing moved, not even the leaves. I walked on.

Crunch, crunch, crunch, crunch.

Then I heard it again. What was it?

I stopped. Waited. Nothing.

Warily watching the edge of the woods, I took a sideways step.

Something brushed my backpack.

"Oh!" I screamed and wheeled around. I saw a wrinkled old face, laughing at me. An old man.

No—a statue. The statue of a dead old man, sitting on top of his grave.

Laughing like a maniac. Laughing at *me*, I thought.

I've got to get out of here. I picked up my pace, *crunch-crunch-crunch-crunch*.

But I heard it again.

A giggle. Or a laugh.

A boy's laugh.

And footsteps—right behind me!

4

I spun around.

No one there.

I listened. Not a sound.

"I've had enough," I murmured to myself. "Facts or no facts, I'm getting out of here!"

I ran out of the cemetery as fast as I could. I passed through another patch of woods and found myself on Fear Street at last, a few steps away from my house.

I sprinted onto the porch, yanked open the door, and slammed it behind me. I tossed my backpack at the foot of the stairs, safely home. The smell of spaghetti sauce drifted out of the kitchen.

I must have imagined those sounds, I thought.

Maybe I heard an echo of my own footsteps. Or the wind in the trees.

"Randy, is that you?" Mom called from the den. "I'm in here with Baby."

"That's *Barbara!*" my little sister shrieked. "From now on everybody has to call me Barbara! No one is allowed to call me Baby anymore!"

"All right, all right," Mom cooed. "It'll take time to get used to it, that's all."

I found my mother and sister watching cartoons together on the sofa. Mom had changed from her nurse's uniform into dark blue sweatpants and a sweater. She's a little chubby, with long brown hair that she always wears in a ponytail. Baby's pale, knobby knees poked out of short denim overalls.

"I'm seven years old!" Baby hollered at me in her shrill, high-pitched voice. "I'm not a baby anymore!"

"I hear you," I said. "You don't have to yell, Baby."

"BARBARAAAA!!!!" Baby screamed.

"Don't tease her, Randy," Mom scolded. "Could you check the spaghetti sauce for me? Just make sure it's not bubbling over."

"From now on call me Clarissa," I joked as I headed for the kitchen. I lifted the lid on the saucepan. The spaghetti sauce smelled great.

"The sauce is fine," I told my mother, settling beside Baby on the couch.

"How was school?" Mom asked me.

"I love my teacher," Baby announced. "His name is Mr. Pine. I'm in love with him!"

"I'm happy for you, Baby, but I'm talking to Randy right now," Mom said.

"That's Barbara!"

"School's okay," I replied. "I've met a lot of nice kids. But a few of them seem weird."

"I'm sure they're nice once you get to know them," Mom assured me.

"I'm going to marry Mr. Pine!" Baby bounced on the couch. "And then I'm going to kiss him!"

"What if he's already married?" I teased.

Baby frowned. "That's impossible. He's mine! Mine mine mine!"

She jumped up and down on the couch like a wild thing. Her shaggy black hair bounced with her. She landed on my thigh.

"Ow!" I cried. "Stop it, Baby! Mom, has she been eating out of the sugar bowl again?"

"Sit down, Baby," Mom commanded. "Look, *Batman*'s on."

Batman was Baby's favorite show. She bounced one last time, landing in a sitting position on the couch.

23

"My name is *Barbara,*" she insisted. "Everybody has to shut up now. *Batman*'s on."

"Why is she so hyper?" I complained. "She acts like a maniac."

Mom patted my knee. "She's excited because of the move and her new school and everything. She'll settle down."

"No talking!" Baby ordered. *"Batman*'s on!"

"Oh, *please,*" I mumbled, standing up. "I'm going to my room. Call me when dinner's ready."

I picked up my heavy backpack and hauled it upstairs to my room. I dropped the backpack on my desk, kicked the door shut, and flopped onto the bed.

From there I could look out the window. My room faced the street. Across the street stood a bunch of two-story houses a lot like ours. One was painted yellow, another pale blue, another a rusty red-brown.

Beyond those houses I saw the beginning of the woods I had walked through. I couldn't see the cemetery, but I knew it wasn't far away.

You heard the wind in the trees, I told myself firmly. Or a squirrel, maybe.

There's nothing to be afraid of in that cemetery.

Nothing to be afraid of at all, I told myself.

Why didn't I believe it?

24

5

"**H**ey, Randy—catch!"

I turned around. A big leather ball hit me in the stomach.

"Ooof!" I clutched my belly. The ball dropped to the floor.

"Sorry, Randy," Sara called. "I didn't mean to catch you by surprise."

I couldn't answer her right away. She'd knocked the wind out of me.

We were in gym class. Ms. Mason, the gym teacher, had gotten out all this old gym equipment and told us to play with it. I guess she hadn't made a lesson plan for that day.

So Sara had heaved the medicine ball at me. It's

like a beach ball made of lead. Tossing it around is supposed to make your arms strong, I think.

But I was tired that day, and kind of a klutz. If I don't get a good night's sleep, I'm completely brain-dead. And I hadn't slept well since we moved to Fear Street.

"Randy? Are you all right?" Sara looked scared now.

I nodded and straightened up. "I'm okay. Maybe we should play with the hula hoops for a while. They look safe."

Sara grabbed a hot pink hula hoop. I took an orange one. I rocked back on one leg and whirled the hoop around my waist. I frantically swiveled my hips.

Shoop, shoop, shoop. The hoop slipped down to my thighs, my knees, my ankles. The little beads rattled inside it as it hit the floor.

I never could hula hoop.

Meanwhile, Sara *shoop-shooped* away.

"How do you do that?" I asked.

"It's easy," she said with a shrug. "You just do it."

I picked mine up and tried again.

Shoop, shoop, shoop, clatter. Straight down to the floor.

"You want to come to my house this Saturday?"

Sara asked me as she hula'd. "I'm having a sleepover."

I was so happy I almost shouted my answer. "Sure! That would be great!"

Maybe at the sleepover I'd get to know some other girls, and soon I'd have a whole crowd of friends.

Laura shimmied past me then, twirling a baton. "Better get in shape, Randy," she murmured. "Or else find a good place to hide."

I glanced at Sara. Her eyes widened.

"She's not going to be at your sleepover, is she?" I asked.

"No," Sara replied.

"Good," I said. "What is she talking about? She said something like that to me last week. Why is she always telling me to watch out?"

Sara let her hula hoop clatter to the floor.

"It's hard to explain, Randy."

"What do you mean, 'it's hard to explain'? Can't you give me a hint, at least?"

I hadn't meant to be funny, but Sara laughed.

"All I mean is it's a long story," she answered. "You'll find out more on Saturday."

I pressed on. "Tell me this much. Am I in some kind of trouble?"

Sara shook her head. "No more than anyone else, Randy. At least I don't think so."

27

Gym class finally ended. Sara and I changed and went to art class. We went to teachers besides Ms. Hartman for a couple of subjects.

We sat at a table with Megan and David and molded wet gray blobs of clay into bowls and cups and saucers.

"Is this play going to be any good, you guys?" Megan asked. "Sherlock Holmes sounds kind of boring to me."

"It's going to be great," Sara told us. "Everyone in it is really good—don't you think, David?"

"Yeah," David agreed, smoothing out the lines of a mug he was making. "Except for Lucas. He's a ham."

"I think Lucas is pretty good," Sara said. She poked dots around the rim of a saucer. "Anyway, his part isn't very big. Basically he gets stabbed by the killer and then lies there while you check out the scene for clues. Playing a corpse should be easy enough for Lucas. How bad could he be?"

"I saw Lucas in his makeup," I put in. "He almost scared me to death."

"He's terrible," David insisted. "All that moaning and shaking. He practically wrecks the play."

"Come on, David," Megan scoffed. "He can't be that bad."

"Okay, he's not that bad," David admitted. "But he's still the worst thing in the play."

"That's probably why he has the smallest part," Sara said.

We all laughed. I felt happy. My second week at school, and I already had some friends. And Sara's sleepover was only two days away.

Sara lived in a big brick house in North Hills. Dad parked out front and went inside with me to meet the Lewises.

My dad's tall and dark-haired and athletic. He wears ugly black-rimmed glasses, but I think he's handsome anyway. He wears jeans and tweed jackets and looks like a professor, but he's really a computer programmer.

Mr. and Mrs. Lewis led us into the living room. Some other parents were sitting there, drinking coffee.

"Welcome to Shadyside," Mrs. Lewis said when she shook Dad's hand. She was tiny and neat. She looked funny next to her husband, who was as tall as Dad. "Sara tells me you just moved here from Maine."

Mr. Lewis handed Dad a cup of coffee and turned to me. "Why don't you take your things down to the basement, Randy? The other girls are already getting settled down there."

Dad leaned over to kiss me goodbye. "Look out for the octopus," he whispered.

He was thinking of the first time I went to a friend's house to sleep over. My friend Tanya's house.

Tanya had weird parents. They served us octopus for dinner.

When Tanya and I got into bed, I kept thinking about the octopus. I felt sure the dead octopus's tentacles were going to reach out from under the bed. They'd grab me and the octopus's ghost would get its revenge by eating me.

I started crying. I called my parents and begged them to come and take me home. Tanya thought I didn't like her anymore.

I was only seven years old at the time. That was before I'd decided not to let my imagination run away with me. Before I realized you have to look at the facts.

You'd think Dad would have forgotten about it by now. I wished he'd let *me* forget it.

"Very funny, Dad," I sniffed.

I carried my sleeping bag through the kitchen and down to the basement.

"Randy's here!" Sara called as I came down the steps.

Our basement is like a dungeon, but the Lewises was all fixed up with a TV and VCR, a stereo, even a kitchenette in one corner. The floor was carpeted,

30

and travel posters covered the walls. Nothing scary about this basement at all.

Sara introduced me to the other girls: Megan, Anita, Karla, and her twin sister, Kris.

I already knew Megan, of course. And I'd seen Anita in gym.

"Spread out your sleeping bag," Sara said. "We're going to make popcorn and watch a horror movie."

I searched for a spot for my sleeping bag. At slumber parties your sleeping-bag spot can be a big deal. Back in Maine, Tanya and I always put ours next to each other.

The other girls had already spread their sleeping bags out over the carpet. Kris and Karla zipped theirs together to make it a double. The sleeping bags formed a rough semicircle in front of the TV. I unrolled my bag in the middle.

Sara made popcorn in the microwave. Mrs. Lewis appeared at the foot of the stairs.

"Having fun, girls?" she asked. "I won't bother you anymore, but you know where to find me if you need me. Don't stay up too late, ha ha."

"Right, Mom," Sara said.

"And try not to make *too* much noise. Sara's little brothers will be going to bed soon. If they can't sleep, I'm going to send them down here to play with you. And I *know* you don't want that."

"She's bluffing," Sara said.

"I am not," her mother replied. "Well, good night, girls. Have a good time!" She waved and tapped her way upstairs in her high-heeled shoes.

"Your mother's so nice, Sara," Kris said.

Sara rolled her eyes. "You should hear her when I come home late."

We all giggled. The timer on the microwave went off, and soon Sara set a big bowl of popcorn beside me.

"What movie are we going to watch?" I asked.

"Dracula," Sara answered.

Kris groaned. "Do we have to watch a scary movie? I get scared really easily."

"You can go upstairs and hang out with my mother if you want," Sara teased. "Since you're so crazy about her."

"Kris, you moron," Karla said. "We already saw *Dracula,* and you said it wasn't scary at all!"

"Oh, yeah. I forgot." Kris smiled sheepishly. She seemed like a nice girl, but kind of spacey. She and Karla looked exactly alike—round faces, big dark eyes, ski-jump noses—except that Karla wore her frizzy black hair short, and Kris kept hers in two thick braids. So far that was the only way I could tell them apart.

We put on our pajamas and settled into our

sleeping bags. Sara slid the tape into the VCR and turned out the lights.

The movie began. It was an old black-and-white version of *Dracula*. I think black-and-white movies are scarier than color—they're so shadowy and dark.

Dracula sank his fangs into his victims' necks. The hair prickled on the back of mine. "It's not real blood," I told myself. "It's only chocolate syrup."

When the movie ended, Sara didn't turn on the lights. We sat and talked in the glow of the television set. The screen showed nothing but fuzz and static now.

"That wasn't scary at all," Kris declared.

"Oh, right," Karla countered. "And you didn't dig your fingernails into my arm the whole time." She flashed her forearm, showing us the marks her sister's nails had made.

"Dracula's not as scary as Pete," Anita said.

The room went quiet all of a sudden. I had that feeling, the feeling I'd had ever since I moved to Shadyside—that everyone knew something I didn't.

I broke the silence. "Who's Pete?"

No one answered.

6

"**W**ho's Pete," I asked again. "Is that the guy with the hockey mask?"

Everybody laughed. But it sounded sort of phony.

"Pete's not a character in a movie," Anita told me. "He's *real.*"

"Real?" I said. "Who is he?"

No one answered right away. The other girls glanced at each other. They wouldn't look me in the eye.

They're just trying to scare me, I told myself. Don't panic. Wait for the facts.

"The tenth is almost here," Kris whispered. "One week from tonight."

The tenth! Not that again.

34

"What's going on?" I demanded. "What's happening on the tenth?"

Silence.

"Why won't anybody tell me?" I wailed.

Still the girls kept quiet. I watched their faces in the gray-blue light of the TV.

"She'll have to find out sooner or later," Anita said.

"Tell me," I insisted.

"It's not fair to keep it from her," Kris said.

Another silence. Sara stood up and got a candle. She lit it and placed it on the floor in the middle of the semicircle. She switched off the TV.

Then Anita spoke.

"Pete was a boy who lived in Shadyside a long, long time ago," she said in a low voice. "He died on his twelfth birthday. He died in the Fear Street Woods."

The candlelight flickered across the girls' faces. They had probably heard the story of Pete a thousand times before, I guessed, but it still held them spellbound.

"No one knows how he died," Anita went on. "His body was found one morning, all shriveled up.

"His parents gave him a funeral. They buried him in the cemetery. They thought that was the end of Pete.

"But one year later—one year to the day after

35

Pete died—some kids were playing hide-and-seek in the Fear Street Woods. All of a sudden a girl started screaming.

"'It's Pete!' she shrieked. 'I saw Pete!'

"The kids ran screaming out of the woods. Pete had been playing hide-and-seek with them."

Anita paused for a long moment.

"One boy left that game completely changed. He began to stay up late at night, howling like an animal. He ran off by himself into the woods. No one knew what he did there. But they knew the boy was not the same.

"Exactly one year later the boy seemed to snap out of it. He stopped going out at night. He stopped going outside at all. He was too scared.

"The boy stayed in bed all day, shaking. His eyes never blinked—he held them wide open all the time, as if he were always terrified. And overnight his hair had turned from dark brown—to white. He looked like an old man.

"A doctor came to examine him. The boy told the doctor that Pete tagged him in the game. And then got to control his body every night. For one year Pete had made the boy do these gross, disgusting things. Pete even made the boy sleep in the cemetery sometimes! Then Pete left.

"No one believed the boy, of course. But then the

36

same thing happened to another kid in town. And the next year, another.

"People began to get scared. Soon no children were ever allowed to play in the Fear Street Woods. But that didn't stop Pete.

"The next year, when no children came to play hide-and-seek on Pete's birthday . . . Pete got angry.

"Pete got very angry. And bad things started to happen. One girl looked in the mirror and saw her face rotting away. Her skin was all green and her teeth were black.

"Another kid kept smelling something, something so putrid that he couldn't eat. Every time he tried, he would gag. He kept getting thinner and thinner.

"Some kids' pets disappeared. Some kids heard a boy yelling 'Ready or not, here I come' over and over until they almost went crazy.

"No one could say for sure that Pete caused the bad things to happen. But they stopped when the kids finally returned to the woods for the game."

Anita stared at Randy with a serious expression on her face.

"Now, every year on the tenth of June, we all celebrate Pete's birthday. We go into the Fear Street Woods and play hide-and-seek. Pete is It.

37

"The first person Pete tags is the loser. Pete takes over his body for the rest of the year. That kid has to watch while Pete does whatever he wants every single night.

"Pete wants a body to live in. A real, live body. He doesn't want to be a ghost. He wants to be alive. Every year he takes a new kid's body. This year it's going to be one of *us!*"

Not one of us moved. I watched the candlelight play on Anita's face. Maybe she was pretending. But she looked scared.

It's just a story, I thought to myself. It has to be.

And I thought Pete was some super-popular kid at Shadyside Middle School!

Sara broke the silence. "That's what the legend says, anyway."

Everyone stared at me, waiting for my reaction.

"Wow," I said. "Um, that's a good story, I guess."

"It's true," Anita insisted. "On June the tenth Pete is going to tag someone we know. Maybe one of us."

"I hope it's not me," Kris said. "I heard Pete makes you run through the woods all night long. He keeps you up all night so you're really tired the next day."

Kris was such a ditz. Karla gave her a punch on the shoulder.

"That's not so scary," I commented.

38

"Well, *I* heard he kills animals and eats them," Sara said. "Remember that time Jeff Walker's dog disappeared? A lot of people thought Pete got him."

"Eeeeyeeew." I was starting to feel a little sick.

Anita pulled a strand of her brown hair out of her mouth. I could tell she believed in Pete and was afraid of him. "He goes to the cemetery at night. And the Fear Street Woods. He howls like an animal. He becomes wild."

"When our grandfather was a kid, his best friend got tagged," Kris told me. "When the year was over, he went crazy. He ended up in an insane asylum."

Karla rolled her eyes. "Only you would fall for Grandpa's old stories, Kris."

"It's true!" Kris insisted.

"My older sister played a few years ago," Anita put in. "She said that after the game this one girl's hair turned completely white, just like in the legend. She looked like a little old lady."

"I heard about a boy who stopped talking completely," Sara said. "Pete took over his body, and the boy never said another word. He just wandered the streets. His jaw shook and his eyes rolled around in his head. He never recovered.

"The things Pete made him do were so terrible . . ." Anita added. "So horrible, he couldn't talk about it. He couldn't talk at all."

39

How awful, I thought. Panic rose in my throat.
But I pushed it down.

Facts, I told myself. These are just stories. You
need facts.

Megan touched my arm and looked me straight
in the eye now. "The thing is, Randy . . . you're in
more danger than the rest of us."

That prickly feeling on the back of my neck
returned. "I am? Why?"

She leaned forward and whispered in a strange,
low voice, "Because Pete likes new kids. That's
why."

The candle flickered, then went out.

A scream cut through the darkness.

7

The basement went pitch-black.

We all huddled together, clutching one another and screaming.

Then, through the screaming, I thought I heard laughter.

Sara must have heard it, too. She said, "Joseph? Paul? Is that you?"

She crawled to a side table and fumbled for the light switch.

The light came on. Against the wall by the stairs crouched two little boys in feetie pajamas. They slumped over, laughing.

"I should have known," Sara huffed. "It's only my stupid little brothers."

They giggled as she chased them up the stairs.

"Just wait till your Cub Scout sleepover!" she shouted after them. "You're going to be sorry! You're going to wish you'd joined the Camp Fire Girls!"

She returned to the semicircle of sleeping bags, scowling.

"Don't yell at them, Sara," Kris said. "I think your little brothers are adorable."

"You can have them," Sara answered. "Take them and Mom, too."

"Should we watch another movie?" Karla asked. "Or maybe there's something good on TV."

"Wait a second," I cut in. "I want to hear more about Pete."

"It's just an old story, Randy," Sara assured me. "You don't have to worry. We were just trying to scare you." She paused. "Right, everybody?"

No one said a word. Anita's big blue eyes watched Sara a little fearfully.

"A-neee-ta," Megan teased. "Only one more week to go."

"People don't tell all these stories about Pete for no reason," Anita insisted. "They're true. I'm sure they are."

"Come on, Anita," Karla said. "You'll believe anything. Remember that time Megan told you her teeth were really dentures? You fell for it!"

Anita's eyes flashed, but she blushed.

"Stop teasing Anita," Sara said. "If you don't believe in Pete, Karla, why are you playing in the game?"

"Why would *anybody* play this game?" I demanded. "That's the part I don't get. I mean, if there's really a ghost named Pete who could take over your body, why take a chance?"

Kris flashed me her dippy smile. "Because it's fun."

"It's not that scary," Megan insisted. "It's kind of cool. Like going to a haunted house on Halloween. You hear about it from the older kids when you're little, so you look forward to it. When you're old enough to play, you get to scare the little kids with it."

"Everybody talks about it afterward," Karla said. "Creepy things happen in the woods, but funny things, too. I'd hate to miss it."

"And if you don't play," Kris added, "everybody thinks you're a wimp."

"You have to play, Randy," Sara said. "Everybody plays."

The other girls laughed.

"Watch out, Randy," Megan murmured. "Pete is going to choose you!"

Karla giggled. "Don't forget—Pete likes new kids, Randy."

"You better practice running," Kris added. "You have to run pretty fast to get away from a ghost."

They all giggled, teasing me and poking me. I pretended to laugh along. But inside I felt worried —and scared.

It's just a game, I told myself. An old tradition.

But what if there were more to it?

"If this legend is true," I began, "that means Pete must be living in some kid's body now. Right? Maybe somebody we know!"

"That's right, Randy," Megan taunted. "Pete could be sitting next to you in school."

"Or in this very basement!" Kris added.

"It could be me!" Sara cried.

"Or me!" Karla said.

"Or me!" Megan shouted, grabbing me.

I yelped. The other girls laughed.

"Randy, watch out! Pete's right behind you!"

Karla pointed and pretended to look scared. The other girls cracked up.

Is any of this true? I wondered. Or are they just trying to scare me?

Facts. That's what I needed.

Cold, hard facts.

I'm going to investigate, I decided.

I'm going to find out the truth.

* * *

44

At school on Monday all I could think about was Pete. And the hide-and-seek game coming up. I passed the bulletin board. More days were x-ed out. Five more days to Pete's birthday.

I kept remembering the stories I'd heard at Sara's sleepover. About how Pete takes somebody's body and uses it at night to do weird, gross things.

Whoever's body he uses, I figured, must be pretty tired all day. I stared into kids' faces, looking for circles under their eyes.

It turned out a lot of kids at Shadyside Middle School looked a little tired. I don't know what *they* were doing all night.

Worrying about Pete, maybe?

I noticed Laura and Maggie glancing around warily. Maybe they're trying to figure out whose body Pete lives in, too, I thought. Laura sneered when she saw me. "You're doomed, new girl," she called.

At least now I knew what she was talking about.

At lunchtime I threaded my way through the crowded halls to my locker. I needed to get my lunch bag.

From halfway down the hall I saw a tall, skinny boy leaning against my locker. Who's that? I wondered.

I think I might need glasses. I don't see too well from far away.

I moved a little closer.

Lucas.

What's he doing? I wondered, approaching my locker. Is he waiting for me?

Why would he be waiting for me? I thought nervously. What does he want?

I took a deep breath and strode over to my locker. He noticed me and straightened up. He *was* waiting for me.

"Hi, Randy."

"Hi, Lucas." I busied myself with my combination lock. I missed the second number and had to start over again.

"Going to lunch now?" he asked.

He leaned against the locker next to mine. He watched me fumble with my lock. He made me nervous. I messed up the combination again.

"Um, yeah," I answered absently. What was my combination again? Twenty-three, five . . .

"So, you want to eat lunch with me?"

I dropped the lock, still unopened.

I studied Lucas's face. Deep blue circles rimmed his eyes.

He looked awfully tired.

"I just thought you might want someone to eat with, since you're new and all. . . ." he added.

The hairs prickled on the back of my neck. *"Pete likes new kids,"* everybody said.

Lucas didn't give up. "Are you going to the hide-and-seek game on Saturday? I really hope you'll be there."

Alarms went off in my head. They started out as tiny clock-radio alarms and grew louder until it sounded like a squadron of police sirens in my brain.

"You have to go," Lucas insisted. "Everybody goes."

Why is it so important to him? I wondered in a panic.

What does he care whether I, the new girl, go to the hide-and-seek game?

I could only think of one reason.

Oh, no, I thought.

Lucas is Pete!

8

Calm down, I told myself.

I leaned my head against my locker and concentrated on the lock. Twenty-three, five, seventeen. Click. The lock opened.

"So, how about it, Randy?" Lucas persisted. "Want to eat with me?"

Don't get him angry, I said to myself. Stay calm—and stay away from him.

I dumped my books in the bottom of my locker. "I can't," I told him.

"Oh. Okay." He drooped a little.

"I promised David and Sara I'd go over the math homework with them," I explained.

Well, it was true.

"David Slater?" Lucas straightened up. "He's such a jerk."

"No, he's not," I said. "He's very nice."

"We'll eat together tomorrow, then," Lucas insisted. "Right?"

"Well—" I hesitated.

"Right, Randy?"

"Sure," I agreed queasily. "Tomorrow."

I watched him slowly walk down the hall toward the lunchroom. A little shiver raced through me. Does the Pete inside him want to tag *me* in the Fear Street Woods?

Stop, I ordered myself. Consider the facts. One: Lucas looks tired. Two: He seems to like me—the new kid. Three: He wants me at the hide-and-seek game.

But that's not enough to prove Lucas is Pete. I'm going to find out for sure, I decided. If I'm positive that Lucas is Pete, I can avoid him at the game.

I won't let him catch me. I don't want to spend the next year with a disgusting boy ghost. Or any ghost at all.

I grabbed my lunch and hurried off to meet David and Sara. I found Sara at a corner table in the back of the cafeteria.

"David's in line getting ice cream," Sara explained.

"Listen, Sara," I said breathlessly. "You've got to help me."

"Help you what?"

"I think Pete has taken over Lucas's body. I'm going to spy on him until I find out for sure. Will you help me?"

Sara stared at me as if I'd gone crazy. "Lucas?" she cried. "No way."

"I think so," I insisted. "You know what he did? He asked me if I'd eat lunch with him."

Sara slapped her hands against her cheeks in mock horror. "He asked you to eat *lunch* with him? That's terrifying!"

I sighed impatiently. *"Listen.* Then he said something about me being *new.* And *then* he said he hoped I'd be at the hide-and-seek game! Plus he looks tired—probably from staying up all night in the graveyard!"

Sara tapped her chin. "I don't know, Randy. It sounds kind of silly to me. I mean, I'm not even sure I believe in all this Pete stuff. We were just trying to scare you at the sleepover."

I wasn't sure I believed in Pete, either. But if there was nothing to the stories, why had they lasted all these years? Why were some kids, like Anita, truly afraid of him? I had to find out—*before* the game.

I nudged Sara. "You won't help me?"

"Help you what?" David sat down, slurping on an ice-cream cone.

"Randy wants to spy on Lucas. She thinks he's Pete."

David laughed. "Lucas? No way."

"That's what I said," Sara pointed out.

I turned to David. "I want to find out for sure, and Sara won't help me. And—well, it would be kind of scary to spy on Lucas alone. Will you help me, David?"

David gaped at me as if I'd lost my mind.

"Come on, David," I pleaded. "It makes sense! If we know who Pete is before the game, we can stay away from him. And you don't want him to tag you, do you?"

"No, I don't," David said. "But what if he catches us spying on him?"

"He won't," I assured him. "We'll be extra extra careful. Please, David?"

He glanced at Sara, who shook her head as if to say, "Randy is nuts and we might as well accept it."

"Okay," David said. "I'll help you."

"Thanks!" I felt better already. "When should we start?"

David shrugged. "How about tonight?"

"You guys are crazy," Sara declared.

"Maybe," I replied. "But when June tenth comes, David and I will know who to hide from. Who knows, Sara—maybe Pete will tag *you*."

I waited until after dinner, when darkness approached.

"I'm going out for a walk around the neighborhood," I told Mom and Dad.

"Can I come?" Baby squealed.

That's just what I need, I thought. Baby tagging along. No way.

"You can't come," I told her firmly. "I want to be alone."

"Be careful, honey," Mom said. "Don't stay out too long."

"I won't," I promised, pushing open the kitchen door.

But secretly I thought, I'll stay out as long as it takes.

I met David on the corner of Fear Street and Park Drive.

"You ready?" he asked.

"Ready," I replied.

We walked to Lucas's house.

Lucas lived on Fear Street, too, not far from my house. We stood across the street, hiding in the shadows. There were lights on in Lucas's kitchen. I saw a woman in the window.

"Who's that?" I whispered.

"Looks like Lucas's mother," David said. "Washing the dishes or something."

We waited. So far the only movement was Lucas's mother in the kitchen window. This could get pretty dull, I thought.

"What if Lucas doesn't come out?" I asked. "What if we waste the whole night standing here for nothing?"

"Shh!" David whispered. "Look!"

The front door opened. Lucas appeared. He hurried down the steps and across the front lawn. He started down Fear Street, toward the woods.

David and I ducked behind a parked car until he passed. Then we followed him. We stayed on the other side of the street. I prayed he wouldn't notice us.

He walked briskly down the street, whistling. The tune sounded familiar.

What *is* that song? I wondered. I know it from somewhere.

He whistled it over and over. At last I recognized it. I remembered singing it as a little kid.

A funeral march. The words went:

Pray for the dead, and the dead will pray for you,
Simply because there is nothing else to do.

I glanced at David. He knew the song, too.

"Creepy," I whispered. "Why is he whistling a funeral march?"

"Maybe it's Pete," David suggested. "Remembering his own funeral."

I shivered.

We passed by my house. I glanced at it longingly. So warm and cozy and safe. Maybe I should run back inside and forget all about this, I thought.

But Lucas kept walking. And David did, too. It was nice of David to come with me. I couldn't let him down now.

And anyway, I had to find out the truth about Lucas.

We reached the Fear Street Woods. Lucas turned off the road and disappeared into the trees.

David and I crossed the street. We hesitated at the edge of the woods.

"It's awfully dark in there," I said.

I heard Lucas's footsteps crunching over the twigs and leaves. They moved deeper and deeper into the woods, and farther away from us.

"We're losing him!" David exclaimed. He started into the dark, dark woods.

My feet didn't seem to want to follow. But I forced them. I didn't want to be alone.

We listened for Lucas's footsteps, trying to follow them.

54

"This way!" David whispered. We shuffled through the shrubs.

But Lucas's footsteps grew faint. After a few minutes I didn't hear a sound.

Where did he go?

I wanted to call out, "Lucas! Where are you!" But I knew that would be stupid. I didn't want him to find us.

We stumbled through the woods, trying not to make noise.

No sign of him now. Lucas had disappeared. He was lost in the shadows.

Then I heard noises off in the distance. I listened hard.

"David! Do you hear that?"

He froze, listening.

It sounded like kids' voices. Kids' voices shouting something.

A breeze fluttered the leaves. The sounds grew clearer, carried on the wind.

I thought I heard a shout of, "Olly olly oxen free!"

There were giggles, and then, "You're It! You're It!"

What's going on? I wondered.

Maybe it's Pete. Maybe he's practicing for the hide-and-seek game!

"I tagged you! You're It!"

I shivered in my shorts and T-shirt. It's June, I

thought. I shouldn't be cold. But the breeze blew across my skin. The hair on my arms stood straight up.

A childish voice screamed, "Run home! Run home!"

David grabbed me by the arm. Sweat dripped down his face. "We've got to get out of here!" he cried.

He yanked on my arm. I didn't have a chance to say a word. We tore through the woods as fast as our sneakers would take us. I could barely keep up with David.

A little boy began to chant. "Five . . . ten . . . fifteen . . ."

"Come on, Randy!" he shouted. "Hurry up!"

I think he was even more scared than I was.

The Fear Street Woods loomed around us like a pitch-black maze. I dodged trees and branches, trying to keep up with David.

"Forty-five . . . fifty . . . fifty-five . . ." the boy called.

Please don't let Lucas spot us, I begged. Please let us get out of here okay.

"This way!" David cried. He pointed to a light up ahead.

"Seventy . . . seventy-five . . . eighty . . ." The boy's voice grew higher and shriller.

I didn't know what the light was. I hoped it meant safety. I aimed my body at it and pumped my legs as hard as they could go.

As I ran, I heard the little boy cry, "One hundred! Ready or not, here I come!"

9

The light swerved past. A car's headlights. It led us safely out of the woods.

David and I stood panting on the curb. Then David started chuckling. A few seconds later he was laughing his head off.

"What's so funny?" I demanded.

David gulped air, trying to catch his breath. "Us!" he gasped. "We got scared of a bunch of little kids!"

He's right, I realized. We heard a bunch of kids playing in the woods and ran out of there screaming bloody murder.

"I'm glad none of our friends saw us!" I said, laughing with him. "We'd never live it down!

"Help! Help! It's a bunch of little kids!"

David pretended to scream. "Oh, no! It's a first grader!"

"Look out!" I joked. "He's got finger paint on his hands!"

"We're too jumpy," David said. "Pete probably doesn't even exist."

"Yeah," I agreed. "We let a stupid story scare us silly."

But inside I wasn't so sure.

The next day Lucas waited by my locker again. Luckily I saw him ahead of time. I turned around and walked in the other direction.

My lunch sat in my locker, guarded by Lucas.

I patted my pockets as I hurried away, wondering if I had any change.

Fifty cents. Enough for an ice-cream sandwich.

I didn't mind. It was better to skip lunch than end up eating raw animals every night.

"Randy, you're starting to scare me," Sara whispered.

"I have to know for sure," I murmured.

We were all gathered on the bleachers in the gym, boys and girls together. Sara and I sat with Kris and Karla.

"Why else would Lucas go into the woods at night?" Sara said. "Either he's Pete, or he's up to something strange. You ought to stay away from him, Randy."

"But I still don't have enough *facts*. Lucas might not be Pete—and I need to know one way or the other before the game. It's only three days away now."

"What are you guys whispering about?" Kris asked.

"Nothing," Sara replied.

"Why won't you tell—" Kris whined.

"What do you think is happening?" Karla interrupted her sister. "We never have gym with the boys."

Usually the girls had gym by themselves. The boys had their own gym teacher, Mr. Sirk.

"I bet we're going to learn judo or something," Kris guessed.

"Like self-defense?" I asked.

"Yes!" Kris's voice rose in excitement. "Maybe we'll learn how to flip the boys over! Wouldn't that be excellent?"

"If only," Karla murmured. "But I can't imagine Ms. Mason teaching us self-defense."

Ms. Mason wore an awful lot of makeup for a gym teacher. Her nails were bright red and always perfectly manicured. If you threw a ball to her, she wouldn't catch it. She'd just let it go—and make you chase it. I guess she was afraid of chipping a nail.

She was careful about her hair, too. She dyed it white-blond and must have used gallons of hairspray on it because it poofed around her head and never moved. She didn't like to go outside on windy days.

She seemed to have other things on her mind besides teaching gym to twelve-year-olds.

"Okay, everybody," she called out, clapping her hands together lightly.

"I think Ms. Mason has a crush on Mr. Sirk," Kris whispered to me.

Mr. Sirk had a weight lifter's build, a head of wavy, glossy dark hair and a mustache. He liked to walk around with his chest puffed out. Mr. Sirk whispered something to Ms. Mason. Ms. Mason giggled.

"See?" Kris gloated.

"Gross," I said.

Ms. Mason clapped her hands again. "I guess you're wondering why the boys and girls are having gym together this week. Well, I'll tell you. We'll be learning something new and different."

"If not judo, then karate," Kris wished aloud. "Please, please, please!"

"Something I think you'll all enjoy," Ms. Mason went on. "Square dancing!"

We all groaned.

Mr. Sirk blew his whistle. "Hey! Let's quiet down now!" he cried sharply.

We quieted down.

Ms. Mason said, "I know you're all excited, but you won't learn anything if you keep talking."

She paused. "Mr. Sirk and I will demonstrate the steps. Then we'll put on a tape of real country music, and you all can try it yourselves. Mr. Sirk himself will be the caller!"

Ms. Mason seemed to think this was very exciting news. No one in the sixth grade got worked up about it.

"First of all, you'll need to choose partners. If you have somebody in mind, go ahead and choose him or her. If you don't have a partner, we'll match you up with somebody."

No one moved, but everyone started talking.

"This should be good," Karla commented.

"I'll bet you anything Laura picks David," Kris said. "You watch."

But no one made a move to pick anyone. Ms. Mason clapped her hands for the zillionth time.

"If you don't want to choose your own partners, Mr. Sirk and I will be happy to choose for you."

"I don't care who I'm with, as long as it's not Jeff Fader," Karla declared. "He's so gross."

Karla, Kris, and I all leaned forward to peek at

Jeff Fader. He sat in the front row of bleachers, picking his nose.

"Yuck!" Kris cried.

Suddenly, from behind us, a girl's voice rang out. "I choose David Slater!"

I turned around. It was Laura.

"What did I tell you?" Kris crowed.

David slumped down on the bleacher and turned dark red. The boys around him slapped him on the back, laughing.

Ms. Mason shouted, "That's the spirit, Laura! Thanks for getting things started. David, you and Laura can come down onto the gym floor. Anyone else?"

For a few seconds no one said a word.

"No one wants to do this dumb square-dancing thing," Karla whispered. "Why doesn't Ms. Mason give up?"

Then, from the middle of the crowd, Lucas shot up.

"I choose Randy Clay!" he called.

10

Lucas chose me!

This time no one laughed or clapped. The bleachers stayed quiet. Kris and Karla stared at me with twin pairs of wide eyes.

From down on the gym floor, David gave me a meaningful look.

Pete likes new girls, they said.

Pete's going to choose *you.*

Lucas chose me.

The facts were adding up.

"All right, Lucas!" Ms. Mason called. "Randy, where are you? Randy is the new girl, right?"

I sat glued to my bench, my legs shaking.

I didn't want to be Lucas's partner. I didn't even

want to learn how to square-dance. But that was beside the point.

"What am I going to do?" I whispered to Kris and Karla.

Karla shrugged. "I guess you'd better go out there."

Lucas made his way down to the gym floor.

"Randy!" Ms. Mason called. "Oh, Randy! I know you're up there somewhere. Come down so we can get things started."

Laura's friend Maggie stood up and pointed at me. "There she is!" she cried. "That's Randy!"

Ms. Mason was losing her patience. "Don't be shy," she chided me. "Hurry up!"

I slowly climbed down the bleachers and stepped onto the gym floor. Lucas stood off to the side, waiting for me.

We'll have to do swing-your-partner, I realized. I'll have to *touch* him. I'll have to touch a *dead person!*

My stomach rolled over. There was no way I'd square-dance with a dead guy.

"Ms. Mason," I said in a weak voice. "I feel sick."

She frowned. "You do look a little pale."

My stomach churned. I really didn't feel well.

"Maybe you'd better go to the nurse's office," Ms. Mason said.

I hurried out of the gym. I felt Lucas's eyes burning into my back as I left.

"You know, it really wasn't so bad, square dancing," Karla said as we emerged from the Division Street Mall. I'd gone to the movies with her and Kris and Sara. It was eight o'clock and not quite dark yet.

"You might have had fun, Randy," Kris added. "We didn't have to talk to our partners or even touch them that much, except when it was time to swing around."

"If anybody had swung me around, I would have thrown up," I said. "I felt sick just looking at Lucas."

"Get over it," Karla scolded. "Lucas ended up dancing with Marcia Lee, and nothing bad happened to her."

"I think you're getting crazy over this hide-and-seek game," Sara agreed. "I mean, no one's really sure if Pete exists."

I bristled. *"You're* the ones who told me about him! And if it's not true, why do you keep playing this game year after year? Why do kids end up in the insane asylum with their hair all white, never to talk again? It has to be true!"

Kris looked scared. "She's right!"

66

"Come on, you guys," Sara said. "The game is just for fun! If it's a little scary, that makes it more fun."

"We know lots of kids who have played," Karla insisted. "And nothing bad has ever happened to them."

All right, I thought. So I'm a wimp. But the more I see, the more I believe Pete exists.

We crossed the mall parking lot and started down Division Street. At Park Drive we split up. Sara, Kris, and Karla caught a bus home to North Hills.

I stood on the corner, waiting for my bus. It didn't come.

After about ten minutes I decided to walk home. It was a warm night, and still light out.

It got dark quickly, though. I began to walk faster. I was late and I knew Mom would be worried. I could hear her scolding me already: "I specifically told you to be home before dark."

Too late for that. It was totally dark now.

But I was almost home. I turned the corner onto Fear Street. Up ahead I saw the Fear Street Cemetery.

I couldn't help wishing I *had* made it home before dark. Passing the cemetery is okay in the daytime, but it's not my favorite place to be at night.

I hurried past, trying not to think about the voices I'd heard there. Trying not even to look at the place.

But something moved near one of the graves. It caught my eye. I couldn't help it. I had to look.

Something white flashed in the darkness. I moved a little closer. I heard the sound of a spade in the dirt. The sound of digging.

A boy crouched near one of the graves. His face was close to the dirt, as if he were sniffing the ground.

I ducked behind a tree to watch.

It was Lucas!

He pulled something out of the ground and held it up in front of his eyes. It was purple and slimy. And I could see it moving. Wriggling and twisting in Lucas's hand.

A worm.

"Yes!" Lucas cried.

And then he did something that made me sure I'd been right all along.

Lucas slowly lowered the fat purple worm toward his mouth.

I started to scream, but stifled it with my hand. A little squeak still came out.

Lucas jerked his head in my direction.

I ducked into the shadows.

Lucas peered through the darkness. He seemed to be sniffing, trying to catch a scent in the air. I held my breath.

Lucas turned away and started digging again.

As quietly as I could, I slipped across the street. I hid behind a tree and peeked at Lucas. Had he seen me?

He kept on digging, face to the ground.

I hurried down the street, keeping in the shadows. I didn't look back until I was safely inside the house.

I poked my head out the door.

No sign of him. I shut the front door and locked it. I was safe—for now.

Pete controls the body at night, I thought. Now it's nighttime. And Pete has taken poor Lucas out to the cemetery.

I shuddered. June tenth is almost here. What if Pete tags me?

Then *I'll* be out in the cemetery at night. Digging up worms. And eating them. I could almost feel a bunch of wriggling, slimy worms in my stomach.

"Randy, is that you?" Mom called from the den. I took a deep breath and went in. Mom, Dad, and Baby all sat in front of the TV, watching a police show.

"How was the movie?" Dad asked. "Are you hungry? We saved you a little chicken if you want it."

"It's warming in the oven," Mom added.

"I had pizza at the mall," I lied.

I'd actually had nothing but popcorn. But I couldn't imagine eating after what I'd seen Lucas do.

"You're a little late, honey," Mom chided me. "Did you have to wait long for the bus?"

"It didn't come," I told her. "I walked home."

Mom and Dad both turned sharply away from the TV to give me their X-ray glares.

70

Dad's voice was low and serious. "You should have called us, Randy. We would have been glad to pick you up."

"I know. I didn't think it would get dark so soon."

Baby jumped off the couch, blocking everyone's view of the TV.

"Oooo," she squealed. "Randy's going to get in trouble!"

"Be quiet, Baby," I grumped.

"Not Baby, Barbara!" she yelled. "Bar-bar-a!"

"Sit down, Baby," Dad said.

"Barbara!"

"I think it's time for bed, Baby," Mom said. "Come on. Let's go up to bed."

Baby let out an earsplitting scream. *"Barbara!"*

Mom held one hand to her ear. With the other she took Baby by the arm and pulled her upstairs.

"Get the tranquilizer gun," I joked.

Dad frowned at me. "Maybe you should go up to bed, too, young lady. I don't like to think of you walking around alone at night."

"I didn't mean to," I said.

"All right," Dad answered. "Go upstairs anyway, and think about it."

I went up to my room. I put on a summer nightgown and snuggled into bed to read. I had to do something to take my mind off Pete. A warm breeze drifted in through the open window, lightly fluttering the curtains.

I don't remember falling asleep, but I must have. I woke up with a start. My bedside lamp was still on. The book had tumbled to the floor. The rest of the house was quiet. What time is it? I wondered.

I glanced at my alarm clock. One o'clock in the morning.

I pulled down my bedsheets and switched off the light. Across the street all the houses were dark. The street was quiet.

Except for a faint sound.

Voices. Voices coming closer.

"I touched you! You're It!"

"He's coming! He's coming! Run!"

"Ready or not, here I come!"

I sat up, shaking.

The voices came from the woods. "Olly olly oxen free!"

I leaned toward the window and stared out. At first I saw no one. And the voices suddenly stopped.

But then something moved under the light of the street lamp.

A boy. A boy darted out of the shadows. He flashed through the pool of light.

I didn't get a very good look at him. He came from the direction of the woods. Then he disappeared down the street. Toward Lucas's house. It had to be Lucas, I thought. Or Pete. I wasn't sure how to think of him.

But I was scared. He's chosen me, I thought. He's after me.

I'm going to be Pete's next body.

12

"**B**e good, girls." Dad kissed me and Baby on the forehead.

"We won't be back too late," Mom said. "If anything happens, call us at the Lewises'." Sara's parents had invited Mom and Dad over for dinner. "I left their number on the refrigerator."

"And don't forget—Baby goes to bed by eight," Dad added.

"Barbara!" Baby protested. "You keep forgetting!"

Dad was busy looking for his car keys. "Sorry, Baby."

Baby pouted and stamped her foot. Sometimes I feel sorry for her. No one ever listens to her.

But then she'll do something obnoxious—like "accidentally" squirting me with her squirt gun—and I wish she'd get kidnapped by aliens. Preferably aliens whose favorite food is seven-year-old girl.

Baby started whining. "I don't want to go to bed at eight. Why can't I stay up late like Randy?"

"You can stay up late when you're Randy's age," Mom said soothingly. "Just think, that's only five years away!"

Baby burst into tears.

"Five years! That's a long time!"

She ran to her room, wailing.

"Thanks a lot, Mom," I said sarcastically. Mom had upset Baby. But *I* had to go calm her down.

Mom leaned down to kiss me goodbye. "Sorry, honey. She'll quiet down soon."

Dad opened the front door. Mom grabbed her purse.

"Say hi to Sara," I called as they settled into the car.

They drove off, waving.

Baby and I were alone in the house for the evening.

I'd baby-sat for Baby before, of course.

But not on Fear Street. Until tonight.

I dragged myself up to Baby's room. Please don't let her go into full tantrum mode, I prayed. Please let her be good tonight.

Being alone with Baby when she's in full tantrum

mode was my worst nightmare. Even Mom and Dad couldn't handle her then.

Once she threw a quart of milk on the floor. The carton exploded like a bomb. Milk splattered all over the kitchen. Another time she tripped me while I was helping Mom clear the table. I was carrying a stack of dirty plates. They fell facedown on the dining room rug. Mom had to take the rug out to get it cleaned.

"Baby?" I called. "How are you doing?"

I listened for a response. Silence. I didn't hear any crying or whining.

Uh-oh, I thought. Is that good or bad?

"Baby?"

I peered into her bedroom.

She wasn't there.

"Baby! Where are you?"

I stepped into her room, searching for her. I checked under her bed. I checked behind the door.

"Baby?"

What could have happened to her?

I pulled open her dresser drawers—she used to hide in there sometimes when she was smaller. Nothing.

"Baby!" I called again.

Maybe she's in Mom and Dad's room, I thought. I turned to leave.

"Boo!" The closet door flew open. Baby jumped out at me.

I yelled. Baby hopped up and down, laughing.

"I scared you! I scared you! I scared you!"

At least it wasn't a temper tantrum.

"Ha ha, Baby," I fake-laughed. "You scared me. Very funny."

"I scared Randy! I scared Randy!"

"Come on," I said, taking her by her little fist. "Let's eat supper."

After a dinner of microwave pizza and ice cream, Baby and I watched TV. I put her to bed at eight-thirty—I always let her stay up late when I baby-sit—and she fell asleep right away.

I collapsed onto the couch in the den. Whew. That wasn't so bad, I thought, relieved. And it'll be a no-brainer from here on.

I couldn't find anything good on TV. I turned it off and curled up on the couch to read a magazine.

An hour passed. It was almost ten o'clock.

I rolled off the couch and went to the window. Outside the world lay dark and quiet.

I stared out toward the Fear Street Cemetery, listening.

Was Lucas in the cemetery tonight? Was he out there somewhere, digging for food?

I checked the front door to make sure it was locked.

All of a sudden I couldn't relax. The house was too quiet. Things didn't feel right.

I paced from room to room. Living room, dining room, kitchen, den.

Maybe I should turn the TV back on, I thought. It will keep me company.

I switched it on. A police show. "Cops to the Rescue."

I thought I heard a noise. In the hall, outside the den.

I froze, listening. On TV, sirens wailed.

Behind me, something clattered to the floor.

I whirled around.

Baby!

She stared forlornly at the plastic plate she'd dropped. Cookies were scattered across the floor.

"I can't sleep," she whined.

"You have to go to bed," I ordered. "Mom and Dad will be home soon, and if you're still up I'll get in trouble."

"But I'm hungry," she cried. A little sob bubbled up from the back of her throat.

Oh, no, I thought. Tantrum on its way.

I stood up, accidentally crushing a cookie under my shoe. I felt like throwing a tantrum myself.

"Come on, Baby," I said irritably. "Help me pick up these cookies. Then you go back to bed."

"You called me Baby again!" she shouted. "I keep telling you! I want you to call me Barbara!"

I blew it! I tried to hold off the tantrum.

"I'm sorry, I'm sorry," I said, trying to soothe her. "I keep forgetting, Baby."

Oops.

She threw back her head and started screaming. At the top of her lungs.

"WWWAAAAAAAAAAAA!"

"Shush! Shush, Baby!"

"WWWAAAAAAAAAAAAAA!"

I grabbed a cookie off the floor and shoved it toward her face.

"Look!" I shouted over her screams. "Look, Baby. A cookie! Don't you want to eat this yummy cookie?"

"WWWAAAAAAAAAAAAAA!"

I shook her. I petted her. I made funny faces at her. Nothing could make her stop. She screamed her head off.

The neighbors will think I'm killing her, I realized.

Then something changed.

She didn't stop screaming. But her screams sounded different.

79

They weren't tantrum screams anymore. They were terror screams.

She grabbed me and pointed toward the window.

"AAAAAAAAAAA!"

I turned to look.

Then it was my turn to scream.

13

"**A**aaaaa! Aaaaaa! Help!" I screamed.

Lucas stared at me through the window.

Then he disappeared. And the front door rattled.

He was trying to get into the house!

I raced to the front door and leaned all my weight against it.

The door's locked, I reminded myself. He can't get in.

Then the lock turned.

"No!" I screamed. "Baby, come help me!"

Baby leaned with me. Tears streaked her face.

The door began to open. I pressed against it.

"*No!*" I yelled. "Go away!"

A mighty shove came from the other side of the

81

door. It flew open, throwing me and Baby out of the way.

"Help!" I shouted. "Stay out! Stay out!"

I hugged Baby, hoping at least to protect her from Lucas.

But Lucas wasn't there.

"Randy! What's the matter?"

I opened my eyes.

Mom and Dad.

I didn't know what to say.

"Randy, are you all right?" Dad demanded.

"I—I—"

"What's going on?" Mom cried.

I felt my cheeks go red and hot.

"Did something happen?" Mom asked. "Was someone trying to get in?"

"Lucas!" I cried. "I saw his face in the window! He's trying to get me!"

Dad frowned. "Who's Lucas?"

"He's Pete!" I replied.

Mom and Dad exchanged baffled looks.

"Isn't Lucas a boy in your class?" Mom asked.

I nodded. I began to realize how crazy I sounded.

Maybe it's better not to tell them, I thought.

What can they do to help me, anyway?

Nothing. They can't do a thing.

"Why would this boy be peeking into our windows?" Dad said. "Maybe I should call the police."

"No—it's okay, Dad," I answered. "I—I probably imagined it."

Mom frowned. "Are you sure, Randy? You seemed awfully frightened."

"I was watching something scary on TV," I lied. "It got to me, that's all."

"I saw him, too!" Baby yelled. "I saw a boy!"

"No, you didn't, Baby," I insisted. "That was on TV."

"It was not!"

"Don't listen to her," I assured Mom and Dad. "You know how she makes things up."

Dad shrugged. "Okay. But if anything else like that happens, let us know."

"I will. I promise."

"I saw him!" Baby cried. "I'm not making it up!"

"Go back to bed, Baby," Mom ordered. "We're all going to bed now."

Dad tried his soothing voice. "That's right, Baby. All us big people are going to bed. Wouldn't you like to be like us?"

"I'm not sleepy!" Baby announced. "I'm wide, wide awake!"

"Well, I guess I'll be going to bed now," I said. "Have fun, you three."

I left Mom and Dad to deal with Baby.

That's it, I thought as I trudged up the stairs.
I've got all the facts I need.
Lucas is Pete.
And Pete will do anything to get me.
Even try to break into my house.
I'm doomed.

14

Crash!

The glass slipped from my hand and smashed on the kitchen floor. Orange juice trickled over the tiles and settled in a crack by the cabinets.

"Rats!" I muttered. I grabbed some paper towels and swabbed at the juice.

"Be careful of the glass, Randy." Mom watched me, frowning. "Are you feeling all right, honey?"

"Sure, sure." I tried to hide my face from her so she wouldn't see how nervous I felt.

Saturday, the tenth of June had arrived.

I'd woken up that morning with a small, hard knot in the pit of my stomach.

The knot grew bigger as the day went on. I tried

to read. I tried to watch cartoons with Baby, but I couldn't sit still. I paced through the house like a caged animal.

"Randy, you're making me nervous," Mom said that afternoon. "Why don't you run out to the store for me? I need a pound of ground beef."

Run out to the store? Did she actually want me to go outside?

"I can't, Mom."

"Why not? It's a perfectly lovely day. You could use some fresh air."

"I really don't feel like it—"

She plunked some money into my palm and pushed me out the door. "Go!" she ordered. "One pound of lean ground beef. Thank you."

The streets seemed oddly quiet for a Saturday afternoon. Usually the neighborhood is full of kids out playing or whizzing around on their bikes.

Not that day. There wasn't much traffic. I saw one man mowing his lawn.

But mostly, I had the feeling people were holed up inside their houses—especially the kids. I imagined them sitting nervously at home, storing up their energy.

They'd need it for the game that night. No one wanted to be tagged by Pete.

No one wanted to be It next year.

* * *

Sara called during dinner that evening.

She almost whispered into the phone. "Don't forget. The game begins just after dark."

"How could I forget? It's all I've been able to think about for weeks."

"Listen, Randy," Sara went on. "Suppose your crazy idea is right. Suppose Lucas really is Pete. All you have to do is stay away from him. He won't be able to tag you, now that you know. . . ."

She's right, I thought. I'll just stay away from him, and I'll be fine.

"I'll meet you there," I said.

"Great." Sara sounded relieved. "See you tonight."

I returned to the table. Baby wolfed down her meat loaf. I wasn't very hungry. But I tried to swallow a few bites of potato. I needed my strength.

I could feel Mom watching me in that worried way out of the corner of her eye. Dad ate cheerfully.

"Big night tonight, huh?" he said to me. "Looking forward to it, Randy?"

I kept my eyes on my plate. "Uh-huh."

"A good game of hide-and-seek. Sounds like fun to me. You'll be part of an old Shadyside tradition."

"Yeah."

"After tonight you'll feel like a true citizen of the town," he went on. "You'll bond with the other kids. It's like an initiation or something."

87

Clearly Dad didn't know what he was talking about. I wished he'd be quiet.

Mom spoke up. "It's not dangerous or anything, is it, Randy?"

"No," I answered in a small voice. I hate lying to my mother. "How could it be dangerous? It's a simple game of hide-and-seek."

"Relax, honey," Dad said. "I'm sure there's nothing to worry about."

"I want to play hide-and-seek," Baby demanded.

"When you're older, Baby," Dad told her. "Your turn will come."

"I want to play now!"

"Behave yourself, Baby," Mom warned. "You want to get sent to bed early?"

"My name is Barbara!"

I set down my fork and watched Baby from across the table. It was weird to think that in a few years she'd be in my place.

She gets on my nerves. But I'd hate to see her controlled by a ghost. She doesn't bother me *that* much.

I pushed my chair away from the table. "May I be excused?"

"You've hardly touched your dinner," Mom noted.

I speared a bite of meat loaf and popped it into my mouth. Just to make her happy.

"I'm full," I replied, chewing. "I'm going upstairs to lie down for a while."

As I left the kitchen I heard Dad saying to Mom, "I'm sure it's nothing, honey. She's probably nervous because she doesn't know too many other kids. Don't forget, she's the new girl at school."

That's right, I thought as I trudged up the steps.

I'm the new girl.

And Pete likes new kids.

We all gathered on the edge of the Fear Street Woods.

This part of Fear Street had no streetlights. Clouds shifted over the half-moon. Some kids carried flashlights. From a distance the lights looked like giant eyes.

My heart raced. I wandered through the crowd of kids my age, hoping to find Sara or Kris and Karla. I peered into people's faces, searching for someone I knew. They stared back at me. Our eyes would meet for a second, then dart away.

I think everyone felt as nervous as I did. No one said much.

Then I saw someone I knew.

Lucas.

He started toward me.

Stay away from me! I silently screamed.

I can't let him near me.

89

I dodged away. I tried to lose myself in the crowd.

I didn't know where I would hide. But it didn't matter. As long as I avoided Lucas.

Mr. Sirk, the boys' gym teacher, stood off to the side. He watched us, his face strangely grim. I wondered why he was there.

Slowly, silently, more kids arrived. We hovered around, expectantly. Everyone kept an eye on Mr. Sirk, as if waiting for some kind of signal from him.

At last he waved his flashlight. We crowded around him.

Mr. Sirk spoke in a low, solemn voice I'd never heard him use before.

"Welcome, kids. As you know, tonight is the tenth of June—Pete's birthday.

"You are here to participate in an old Shadyside ritual: a game of hide-and-seek.

"Generations of Shadyside kids have played. You are following in the footsteps of your parents and grandparents. After tonight none of you will be the same."

Mr. Sirk gave a creepy mad-scientist laugh. A couple kids snickered, but most didn't even smile.

We listened to every word he said, more quietly and more obediently than we ever did at school.

"For the majority of you, the game will be just that—a game," Mr. Sirk went on. "But for one of you, there is a great deal at stake. I think you all know what I mean."

My stomach flipped. Not me. Don't let it be me.

"The rules are simple: No flashlights allowed. You'll leave your flashlights here by the road.

"At the signal you'll run into the woods to hide."

We all turned our eyes to the woods. They stood deep, dark, and silent, ready to swallow us.

He patted a huge, gnarled old tree. "This is home base. If you touch it on your way out of the woods, you're safe. But you must stay in the woods and hide for at least half an hour. No one is safe before half an hour passes."

He paused. None of us moved. We waited to hear more. My heartbeat throbbed in my ears.

At last Mr. Sirk spoke again. "I guess you all know who's It."

No one said a word. We all knew.

It was Pete's birthday. Pete was It.

Mr. Sirk cleared his throat. "Good luck to you all. And please be very careful."

Someone struck a match. In the glow I saw Sara's face. She lit twelve candles. Twelve candles on top of a big birthday cake.

Two girls I didn't know helped Sara lift up the cake. The candlelight threw weird shadows on their faces.

Across the top of the cake, scrawled in red frosting, I saw the words "Happy Birthday Pete."

Everyone began to sing.

"Happy birthday to you."

I'd never heard "Happy Birthday" sung so grimly. But then, I'd never been to a birthday party for a ghost before.

I joined in. We sang very slowly.

We're all secretly trying to put this off, I thought. To put off playing this game for as long as we can.

The song ended. Everyone stood still as statues, waiting.

Waiting for what? I wondered.

What is the signal?

I saw Sara's mouth twitch nervously in the candlelight.

Suddenly the candles went out.

Only I didn't see anyone blow on them.

The woods were pitch black.

The game had begun.

15

Everybody ran.

Sara and the other girls dropped the cake. *Splat!* It smashed in the dirt. Kids trampled it as they raced into the woods.

We all spread out. Sara glanced back and saw me. She beckoned me to follow her.

I shook my head. Pete would find two of us more easily than one.

I stopped a few yards into the woods. Which way to go?

I heard footsteps behind me and turned. A boy ran straight for me.

Lucas!

No. Another boy. He brushed past me and disappeared behind a tree.

No sign of Lucas. Safe for now.

I scurried along a narrow path, deeper into the woods. Kids ran everywhere. I heard shrieks and laughter and screams all around me.

No one had found a place to hide yet. I had to get away from them. I had to go deeper into the woods.

I peered through the darkness as I ran. My feet crunched on the low shrubs. My thoughts raced.

Quiet! I scolded myself. You've got to be silent! Where can I hide?

These woods are huge, I realized. I felt lost in them.

All the other kids seemed to have disappeared. I kind of wished I'd see someone I knew. Sara or Kris or somebody. Anybody but Lucas.

I˙ pushed on into the woods. I'm all alone, I thought.

No. I'm not alone.

Crunch crunch crunch.

I tried to listen. My heartbeat pounded in my head. I stood still.

Twigs crackled. Footsteps behind me.

I glanced back. Who's there? I didn't see anyone.

But I heard someone.

Crunch crunch crunch.

Getting closer.

Maybe it's Sara, I wished. Or some other friend. But the longer I stood still the more scared I felt.

I took a deep breath. I can't wait to find out who this is, I realized. I have to get away!

I started to run again. I ran faster.

Crunch crunch crunch.

Closer. Closer.

I swerved off the path, hoping the footsteps wouldn't follow. I crashed through bushes and low branches.

Crunch crunch crunch.

Headed right for me. Still closer.

Someone was chasing me!

16

I whirled around.

Lucas?

No.

No one.

The footsteps had stopped. There was no one behind me.

Forget it, I told myself. Keep running.

I plunged blindly through the woods. I dodged the trees in my way. Branches snapped in my face, stinging my eyes.

I came to another path. I paused.

Crunch crunch crunch.

There they were again. The footsteps!

I spun around.

The crunching sounds stopped.

I strained my eyes, staring through the darkness. No one there.

I wish I had a flashlight, I thought. Why aren't we allowed to have flashlights?

No time to worry about it. I turned onto the new path and raced on.

I stumbled over rocks and roots, panting. I can't run much farther, I realized.

I've got to rest.

The footsteps kept getting closer, closer.

They'll catch up to me soon.

I've got to hide. But where?

Nothing around but trees. Got to hide in a tree.

I grabbed the nearest branch and pulled myself up.

I climbed as high as I could. The bark scraped my hands. I settled in a crook of the tree, catching my breath.

I stared down. I should have picked a taller tree, I thought. Maybe then I could spot Lucas coming.

Now I can't see anything but leaves.

At least they'll hide me well.

Pete won't find me. He'll never see me up here.

I sat for several minutes, perfectly still.

Not a sound in the woods.

What happened to those footsteps? I wondered.

And how much time has gone by? Ten minutes? Fifteen?

How will I know when half an hour has passed?

I wish I had a glow-in-the-dark watch.

No. Pete would see it for sure.

I clung to the branch, waiting.

The tree began to shake.

I froze.

Stay calm, I told myself.

It's the wind. It must be the wind.

I hadn't heard any footsteps. I hadn't heard anyone approach.

So it has to be the wind. Right?

The tree shook harder. Too hard. And I didn't feel any breeze.

It wasn't the wind.

My mind raced. Stay here! Stay here!

I'm safe here. I *must* be!

But all at once I knew I wasn't safe.

I knew it. I felt it.

Hot breath on my neck.

Someone was in the tree with me.

Right next to me.

So close he could touch me.

17

I was afraid to look. But I had to.

I twisted my head around.

A boy! A boy sat beside me in the darkness.

Not Lucas.

David.

Blond David in a white T-shirt. It was easy to see his pale hair and pale shirt in the faint moonlight.

I started to breathe again.

What a relief. It was only David.

"Hi," he whispered. He shifted, and the branch shook.

"Shhh!" I hissed. "Careful! You're making too much noise."

I was glad to have him there, though.

Maybe I was wrong to try to hide alone, I thought. It's too scary.

It felt better to have company.

"Don't worry, Randy," David said. "Pete won't get you as long as you're with me."

I smiled. David's nice, I thought. He's really the best person who could have turned up.

He spied on Lucas with me. He understands how scary it is.

"I'm glad you're here, David," I whispered. "We'll be safe now."

He nodded. "Everything's going to be fine."

We sat in silence for a long time, waiting.

"Maybe we can make a break for it soon," I murmured. "We can run for home base together."

"Soon," David answered. "Not yet."

The woods were completely silent. I felt good. It was almost over.

Then I noticed a funny smell.

The faint odor of garbage.

I sniffed.

Or maybe rotten vegetables?

Where was it coming from?

The smell grew stronger.

"Do you smell something?" I asked. "It's gross."

David shook his head. "I don't smell any-thing."

"Funny," I said. The odor grew worse by the second. I began to feel a little sick to my stomach.

"It's as if we're hiding in a garbage truck," I said. "Worse, even."

David shrugged.

And then I realized—the smell came from David.

David smelled funny.

David smelled *horrible*.

At first I felt embarrassed.

I shouldn't have said anything, I thought.

Maybe he forgot to take a bath or something.

But the smell kept getting stronger.

Worse than someone who never takes a bath.

Worse than fifty garbage trucks.

I choked. I wanted to hold my nose. But that would have been rude.

I studied David more closely.

His white shirt had a stain on it. A dark stain the size of a quarter, right on his chest. I didn't think much of it.

But when I looked at him again, the stain had grown. Now it was as big as a CD.

He smelled bad and his shirt was stained. I never knew David was such a slob.

I pointed to the stain.

"What happened?" I asked. "Did you spill something?"

101

"In a way," he answered.

Strange. Now his voice sounded funny, too.

Not quite right. Not like David's usual voice. A bit higher.

Without thinking, I slid away from him a little.

"This game's so stupid," David said. His voice changed more.

"Pete's not so bad. I don't know why everybody tries so hard to get away."

The voice had completely transformed now. Not David's voice at all.

I sat frozen in the tree, staring at him. The stain spread across his shirt, slowly growing bigger.

"What is everybody so afraid of?" the boy beside me demanded. "Pete always gives the bodies back.

"I give them back as good as new."

Alarms shrieked in my head.

I.

He said *I!*

The boy smiled at me. He didn't look like David anymore.

His teeth were crooked, rotten and black.

His breath blasted me in the face, hot and stinking.

And the stain on his shirt began to drip.

Drip, drip.

A drop fell onto my hand. I held my hand up to my eyes and stared at the drop.

Dark red. Warm.

Blood.

He was Pete!

18

"**D**on't worry, Randy," Pete croaked. A decayed tooth fell out of his mouth as he spoke.

"It won't hurt a bit. It's not so bad to let me take over your body.

"Think about it—you'll never be lonely."

I didn't wait around to hear more. I scrambled out of that tree as fast as I could.

The bark scraped my hands, but I didn't care.

"Don't run," Pete called after me. "I'll catch you. You can't get away from me."

I jumped out of the tree. I fell ten feet, landing on the soft dirt below.

Then I sprang up and raced for home base.

I didn't look back.

I didn't have to. I could feel Pete's hot, stinky breath on the back of my neck.

I stumbled through the woods. Branches clawed at me. I slapped them away.

Pete's heavy footsteps pounded behind me.

I had no time to think about which way to go. I ran.

I hoped I was headed for the edge of the woods.

I had to get to home base. If I could tag that oak tree, I'd be safe.

I heard Pete's voice, almost in my ear.

"It's hopeless, Randy," he called. He wasn't panting or out of breath. I guess ghosts don't get tired.

But I knew I couldn't run much longer.

Where was that stupid oak tree?

Then I heard voices.

Kids' voices.

I swerved toward them.

I saw it.

The edge of the woods. Home base.

Kids stood by the oak tree, waving flashlights.

"Hurry!" they called. "You're almost home!"

"You won't make it!" Pete's voice cried. "Give up now, Randy. You can't beat me!"

No! No, no, no!

I won't give up. I won't.

I'm going to make it home.

The tree stood only a few yards away. I held my
arms out in front of me, reaching, reaching . . .

Something caught my foot.

I stumbled and lost my balance.

I fell flat on my face.

I was trapped.

19

"No!" I screamed.

He's got me. He's going to take my body. Would it hurt?

I scrambled to my feet. Pete reached out to tag me, his fingers less than an inch from my arm.

"Hey, Pete!" a familiar voice called. "What are you going to do? Spend a whole year in a *girl's* body?"

Pete hesitated. He turned and peered into the woods.

Lucas appeared between two trees, dancing around like a boxer. He laughed. "A girl named Pete—that's a good one! We'll have fun all year teasing you about that!"

Pete stared at him, growling like an animal.

"Come and get me, Pete!" Lucas taunted. "Or should I say 'Petina'!"

Lucas disappeared behind the trees. "Do you have to pick on a girl, Pete?" he yelled. "Afraid you can't catch a guy?"

Pete tore after him.

"Go, Lucas!" I screamed. "You can do it!"

A boy in a green T-shirt cut in front of Pete. Charging toward home base.

Pete turned and lunged toward the boy. He missed. He spun around and headed back in the direction we had seen Lucas.

I realized I hadn't tagged home. I threw myself at home base. I didn't just touch the tree—I hugged it.

I was safe. Safe forever. Or at least for a whole year.

But what about Lucas? I stared around the woods, searching for him. I heard someone crashing through the bushes. Did Pete catch Lucas? Or had Lucas found a new place to hide?

I can't believe how wrong I was, I thought, panting.

Lucas wasn't Pete. It was David all along. And I asked him to help me spy on Lucas!

Kids still darted through the woods. I clutched the tree, safe, listening to their shouts.

Who was Pete chasing now?

Sara suddenly appeared, dashing for home. She slammed against the tree.

"You made it!" I cried, hugging her. "We're safe!"

She nodded, catching her breath. We hung around, waiting for other kids to come in.

Megan appeared, and then Karla and Kris. I watched for Lucas, but I didn't see him.

A good sign, I thought. The longer he's out, the more likely it is he got away from Pete.

"That was fun!" Kris exclaimed. "It wasn't scary at all."

"Sure," Karla joked. "You weren't scared. You only screamed every time I touched you."

"Well, you could have been Pete!" Kris protested.

"Pete almost got me," I told them. "But Lucas saved me!"

"Lucas?" Sara sounded confused. "But you said he was Pete."

"He wasn't," I explained. *"David* was!"

"No way," Megan shot back. "You're making that up, Randy."

"I am not! David was Pete! He chased me, but Lucas saved me just in time!"

"I'm sure David was just having fun with you," Megan insisted. "He's *not* Pete."

"He is!" Why wouldn't they believe me?

"Okay, Randy. We believe you." Sara rolled her eyes, and the other girls giggled.

"Ask David," I demanded. "He'll tell you."

We glanced around, but there was no sign of David.

"You'll call him tonight and get him to go along with your story," Megan said.

"You'll see," I told them. "Monday morning David will come into school with gray hair or something. Then you'll believe me."

"I'll believe you got him to dye his hair somehow, that's what I'll believe," Karla teased.

More kids sprinted out of the woods and tagged the tree. They milled around with their flashlights, talking and laughing.

Mr. Sirk blew a whistle. "Game over!" he announced. "Until this time next year."

Everyone clapped and cheered. We were all so happy the game was over. Kids started to wander away in groups of twos and threes.

"Has anyone seen Lucas?" I asked.

"I saw Lucas as I was running for home," Kris answered.

"Was he all right?" I asked her.

Kris shrugged. "He looked fine to me."

"He probably tagged home while we were talking and then left," Sara suggested.

Good, I thought. Lucas is okay. Maybe Pete couldn't catch anyone this year.

I've got to apologize to Lucas, I decided. And thank him.

And explain why I avoided him all this time.

More kids headed out of the woods. People waved their flashlights. "See you next year, Pete!"

I said goodbye to Sara and Kris and Karla. I walked home alone. It had been a terrifying night. But it's over now! I thought.

Even alone in the dark I don't feel afraid. I don't feel afraid of anything anymore! I felt so happy.

No more Pete!

On Monday morning I strolled through the crowded halls, keeping an eye out for Lucas. I didn't find him, so I went to class.

"I hope you and David got your stories straight," Megan teased.

"He'll back me up," I insisted. "You'll see."

But David never showed up. The first bell rang and Ms. Hartman closed the door. David's seat was empty.

Where was he?

A boy whispered something to Megan. She passed it along to me.

"Somebody heard David had to go to the hospital," she whispered. "Do you think—?"

I nodded. Poor David.

* * *

111

Sara and I passed the baseball field after school that day. Shadyside was playing Hartsdale. I hadn't seen Lucas all day. I couldn't wait to talk to him.

We settled in the bleachers to watch. Lucas stood on the pitcher's mound. He whizzed the ball past the Hartsdale batter.

"Kris said she heard David's okay," Sara told me. "He's supposed to get out of the hospital tomorrow."

"What's wrong with him?" I asked.

"I don't know. Some kind of virus or something . . ."

"I'm telling you he was Pete! That's what made him sick."

"Okay, okay."

"Strike three!" Lucas struck out the first batter. Sara and I clapped.

"What are you going to say to Lucas?" Sara asked as we watched the game.

"I'm not sure," I replied. "I guess I'll explain that it was a misunderstanding. It sounds kind of silly now."

Shadyside beat Hartsdale five to three. I hung around, waiting for Lucas to come off the field.

Sara nudged me. "I guess you want to thank him by yourself. Call me and let me know what happens."

"Okay," I agreed.

She gave me a playful little wave and dashed off.

Lucas ambled off the field. He carried his bat over one shoulder. His baseball mitt hung off the end of it.

"Hi," I said.

"Hi," he said back. He smiled. "That was some game of hide-and-seek the other night, wasn't it?"

"Yeah," I agreed.

We began to walk toward home.

"Are you all right?" he asked. "You didn't get hurt or anything, did you?"

"I'm fine," I answered. "How about you? Are you okay?"

"Great." He grinned.

He took off his baseball cap and pushed a lock of curly dark hair off his forehead.

He's really cute, I thought. Why didn't I notice that before?

I took a deep breath. Apology time.

"Lucas—I can't believe what you did for me. Pete would have gotten me for sure if it weren't for you."

"No big deal." He put his cap back on, shrugging.

"It's a big deal to me. Especially since—well, I guess I haven't been very nice to you."

"You kept running away from me," he said. "I did kind of notice that."

113

"Well, you know, I can explain," I stammered. "See, I thought—"

I paused.

"It seems so stupid now I'm embarrassed to say it."

We crossed the street. He looked at me, waiting to hear what I had to say. His expression was so friendly I decided to go for it.

"Um, I thought you were Pete."

Lucas laughed. "You thought *I* was Pete? Why?"

This part was embarrassing, too. Should I admit that David and I had spied on him?

No, I decided. I may like to *get* all the facts, but that doesn't mean I like to *give* them all.

"Well," I began, "one night I happened to be passing by, and I saw you in the cemetery. You were digging worms, and I thought Pete was looking for food."

Now Lucas laughed really hard.

"So," I went on, "what were you doing?"

"I was digging worms. You know, night crawlers? But not to eat. To use for fishing bait."

"Oh." I laughed with relief. "Fishing. Why didn't I think of that?"

Then I remembered another strange thing.

"Can I ask you something else?" I began. "Did you come to my house one night and look through the window? I was sure I saw you—"

He laughed again. "I did. I was passing your house on my way home from digging night crawlers, and I heard this terrible screaming—"

Screaming? Oh, yes. Of course.

Baby.

"And I thought maybe you were in trouble. I saw a light on and ran to the window to make sure you were all right."

"Then my parents came home," I finished for him. "And what happened to you?"

"I felt weird about peeking through your windows, so I ran away."

We turned onto Fear Street, both laughing. The sky instantly darkened. I'd noticed that happened a lot on Fear Street.

I paused for breath. Lucas kept laughing.

He laughed harder and harder. His laughter began to sound weird to me.

Not so jolly and happy. More raspy and harsh, as if he had a cold or something.

I glanced at him. His face looked strange. Distorted.

His mouth twisted into a crooked grin. Or was it a scowl?

The trees are throwing shadows on us, I thought. That's why he looks creepy.

He squinted at me, his eyes glittering.

"You know," he rasped, "Pete really wanted you."

115

My heart began to pound.

There is no reason to be afraid of Lucas now, I ordered myself.

"You got away from him." Lucas's voice sounded angry. "That wasn't supposed to happen."

"What?" I didn't understand.

Then I smelled something bad. Rotten.

That same rotten odor I smelled in the woods.

I stared at Lucas. His face twisted horribly now. His mouth pulled into a tortured grimace. His eyes bulged and crossed. The skin on his cheeks tightened over the bones.

He opened his grotesque mouth to speak. His rotten breath blasted into my face.

"It wasn't fair!" he yelled. "I really wanted you!"

He grabbed me.

"No!" I screamed.

Pete!

20

His hand gripped my arm, his fingers digging into my skin. I didn't care. I ripped my arm away and ran.

"You can't get away from me!" he shouted. "I'm going to get you! I don't want Lucas—I want you!"

No way! I thought. But I didn't waste any breath yelling it. I turned in the direction of home and ran.

I had to take the shortest way. I didn't care if I had to run through other people's yards, or through the woods, or—

The cemetery. The Fear Street Cemetery.

I was headed straight for it.

I can't turn away now, I thought. It's the fastest route home.

I glanced back. Pete was speeding toward me. If I paused for one second—*bam!*—he'd catch me!

I didn't hesitate. I raced through the cemetery gates.

Stay calm, I told myself. Just cross through the cemetery. Then you'll be safe.

Behind me Pete's footsteps echoed closer and closer.

"Give up, Randy!" he yelled. His stinky breath washed over me. "Pete likes new kids. . . ."

I pumped my legs harder. I nearly tripped over a headstone. I dodged it. I jumped over another one. I trampled over the graves, crushing old dead flowers underfoot.

Then a hand reached up—up out of a grave—and grabbed my ankle.

21

I wrenched my ankle free. I glanced back.

There was no ghostly hand. Just a vine of ivy straggling across the path.

And pounding closer, Pete's heavy steps.

I jumped to my feet and started running again.

Don't worry about the graveyard, I scolded myself. Don't worry about ghosts. There are no ghosts.

Except Pete.

And that see-through girl standing in front of me.

What!

See-through girl?

She opened her mouth and blasted me with icy breath.

"Home base is the other way!" she shrieked.

I stopped dead.

A ghost girl!

I started to turn around. But the other way led to Pete.

Trapped!

And then I heard them.

The sounds that had been haunting me at night. "Olly olly oxen free!"

Childish voices shrieked all around me. "Ready or not, here I come!"

One by one they rose from their graves. Ghost children. Pale, white, nearly transparent. Girls and boys of all ages. All dead. All ghosts, icy cold.

"You're It!" they screeched. "You're It!"

They crowded around me, howling and moaning. Their ashen faces were small and sweet, but twisted with anger. They wore old, tattered clothes—long dresses with torn skirts and schoolboy knickers rotting apart.

What are they going to do to me?

The screaming grew louder, their breath icier.

I shivered in the sudden chill. I scanned the cemetery, searching for a way to escape.

They pressed in, closer, closer.

Anyone around our base is dead, they shrieked.

I covered my ears against their shrill voices.

I spun around. Pete leaned against a tree, watching me. I was trapped!

One of the ghost boys noticed Pete. "You loser!"

the ghost boy yelled. "Not good enough to play with us, right, Pete? Stupid humans are the only ones you can beat!"

The ghost children danced by me, taunting me. "You can't get away now! Oh, no, you can't get away!"

"Try to escape," a dead girl whispered. "I dare you!"

"Help!" I screamed. "Help!"

But the ghost voices grew louder and shriller, covering my screams with their own.

"Five, ten, fifteen, twenty . . ."

No one would hear me.

No one would save me.

Pete was ready to pounce on me if I ran.

The ghosts moved closer and closer.

They closed in on three sides of me. Pete waited behind me.

"Forty-five, fifty, fifty-five . . ."

They're counting to a hundred, I realized.

And then what will they do?

What happens when they get to one hundred?

"Ninety, ninety-five—

"One hundred!"

That's it, I thought.

It's all over.

No, I ordered myself. Don't give up.

"Hey!" I yelled as the ghosts flew at me. "I thought only loser ghosts played with humans. You are no better than Pete."

"Pete's a loser!" a ghost boy shouted.

"Loser! Loser!" the others taunted.

"Yeah. Pete is a loser!" I yelled. "He couldn't even catch me—a human—in the hide-and-seek game last night!"

Pete howled in fury.

"You cheated!" he shrieked. "But I'm still going to win!"

Pete lunged at me, but the boy ghost slid between us, chanting,

> "Pete, Pete,
> Smell my feet.
> Give me something
> Good to eat!"

More ghosts circled around Pete.

"Stop playing with stupid humans, Pete," a girl chided.

"Yeah, Pete!" screeched another ghost. "You're such a loser."

"What's the matter? You afraid of us, Pete?"

"You don't seem so scary now, Pete," I taunted. "You're afraid to leave that human body, aren't you?"

I could see Pete. The ghosts whipped around him. Pete's face popped out through Lucas's. His mouth twisted with anger. His eyes bulged.

One of the ghost children tweaked his nose, and Pete jerked his head back inside Lucas's body.

"Pete, your mom says get out of that body and back into your grave—right this minute!" the ghost girl teased.

"Are you too scared to play with us, Pete?" they shouted. "You have to pick on stupid human kids?"

Most of the ghosts stopped paying attention to me. They circled faster and faster around Pete. Slowly I began to inch away.

A ghost girl shouted, "Hey, Pete—catch!" She plucked off her head, bonnet and all, and tossed it at Pete. He caught it and stared at it, horrified. The disembodied head giggled and flew back on top of the girl's neck.

I forced myself not to scream. I didn't want the ghosts to turn on me.

A boy stuck his face in Pete's and blew out his icy breath. Pete shivered. A little beard of icicles formed on his chin.

"You're It, Pete!" they chanted. "You're It, you're It, you're It!"

Lucas's body began to shake. It quivered, faster and faster.

What's happening?

For a few seconds I saw two bodies—Lucas's and another boy's. Pete's smelly, rotten-toothed body. Messy hair, freckles, dressed in ragged old clothes. But clear and filmy, like the ghosts'.

Then Pete pulled himself back into Lucas.

"I won't come out!" Pete cried.

If I ran now, I could get away.

No, I thought. I have to save Lucas.

"I knew you were afraid, Pete!" I screamed. "You are afraid of the other ghosts. You are even afraid to come after me unless you are safe in someone else's body!"

"Yeah!" the ghost children shouted.

"If you won't come out yourself, we'll suck you out!" a ghost child declared.

The ghosts spun around Lucas and Pete. I watched them whirl around like a cold, white tornado.

"No!" Pete cried. "I want to stay with the humans!"

The spinning ghosts laughed.

"They're too easy to beat!" one shouted.

"Don't be a wimp. Play with us!"

Pete's freckly face rose out of Lucas's head. Then his neck was sucked out, and his torso and legs. With a loud *thwock!* the white whirlpool yanked Pete's body away and up into the air.

124

He struggled as he spun around like laundry in the rinse cycle.

They sucked him away, back into the cemetery.

They sucked him down, down into a grave.

A grave marked PETER JONES.

"I want to play with Randy!" he protested. Then his head was sucked below the ground.

Laughing, the other ghosts returned to their graves. I thought I heard one of them say, "Pete's a spoiled brat. He wants to be It all the time!"

22

The icy wind died. Lucas and I found ourselves standing alone in the silent graveyard.

No sign of the ghosts. No sign of Pete.

It was as if nothing had happened. Except to Lucas.

I stared at him. His face had turned pale, almost green.

But was he really Lucas again? Or still Pete?

I sniffed him warily. No bad smell. He was his old Lucas self again.

"Are you okay?" I asked.

He patted his hair, trying to make it go back to normal.

"I'm okay, I guess," he replied. "Whew. Thanks for saving me from Pete."

"I owed you one," I told him. I scanned the graveyard once more. All the ghosts were gone. And Pete, too.

"Let's get out of here," I suggested.

Lucas took my hand. We walked out of the cemetery on shaky legs.

"You know," he said, "hide-and-seek is a real baby game."

"Yeah," I agreed. "We're way too old for it."

"We sure are," Lucas declared. "I'm never playing hide-and-seek again."

"Me, neither."

And I never did.

GHOSTS of FEAR STREET ®

SPELL OF THE SCREAMING JOKERS

SPELL OF THE SCREAMING JOKERS

"This whole mess is Frankie Todaro's fault and—oowww!" I howled. "That hurts, Louisa!"

"Sorry, Brittany. But you know—looking great isn't easy. Just read those magazines." Louisa pointed to a stack of my magazines piled high on the floor. "They all tell you that."

"Then I won't look great," I said, yanking her curling iron out of my hair.

It was Saturday afternoon. My best friend, Louisa Wong, had come over to my house. She was always trying out ways to improve my short brown hair. So far, none of them had worked.

"Besides," I went on, "I don't care what I look like for this dumb community-service thing."

1

"Bad attitude, Brit," Louisa told me, shaking her head.

Louisa is into fashion. That day she had on a lavender baby T-shirt, a long silky skirt, and navy blue nail polish.

I had on a pair of old jeans and a Shadyside Middle School sweatshirt. I'm into comfort.

I flopped down on my bed. "You know," I went on, "if Frankie hadn't make us look at his dumb pet rat, none of this would have happened."

"I thought he was cute," Louisa said.

"Who?" I raised my eyebrows. "Frankie?"

"No!" Louisa cried. "Spike!"

"Spike—cute? I guess—if you're into albino rats. Why did Frankie bring him to school anyway?"

"Somebody dared him to put Spike on Mr. Bladvig's music stand." Louisa shrugged. "You know how he is."

"Who?" I asked. "Spike?"

"No!" Louisa laughed. "Frankie! You know how he loves dares."

I shook my head. "I barely know Frankie."

"He was in my class last year," Louisa told me. "Trust me, he'll do anything."

BANG!

Louisa shrieked as my bedroom door flew open. My little brother crashed into my room.

2

"Jimmy!" I yelled. "You're supposed to knock. Remember?"

"Pick a card!" Jimmy demanded. He charged over to me, waving a deck of cards. "Come on, Brit! It's my new trick! Pick a card!"

I groaned. I'm not crazy about cards to start with. Then Mom and Dad bought Jimmy a card-trick book for his eighth birthday. Ever since, he's been a total pain.

I was really, really sick of his card tricks. "Ask Louisa to pick," I told him.

Jimmy fanned the cards. Louisa picked one. She showed it to me. Six of clubs.

"Now put your card back in the deck," he instructed her.

Louisa slid the card back into the pack.

Jimmy shuffled. "Okay, pick the first four cards."

She did. "Hey!" she cried. "They're *all* sixes!"

"Tah-dah!" Jimmy took a bow.

"How'd you do it?" Louisa asked, handing him back the cards.

Jimmy grinned. "Magicians never tell," he declared. He turned to me. "Your turn, Brit. Pick a card! Any card!"

"Not now," I said. "We have go to Max David-son's house."

"Who is he?" Jimmy asked. "Your new boy-friend? Are you in *loooove* with him?"

3

"I've never even met him," I snapped. "He moved to Shadyside last week. But he's sick, so he can't come to school."

Jimmy wrinkled his nose. "What's he got?" he asked.

"Rabies, for all I know," I said glumly.

"Brit!" Louisa cried. "You're horrible!"

"Why do *you* have to go see him?" Jimmy asked.

"Because Max's mom asked the principal if some Shadyside kids could visit him. So Mr. Emerson picked us."

"Oh." Jimmy cocked his head to one side. "Why did he pick you?"

I sighed. He wasn't going to give up.

"We got in trouble for looking at a rat," Louisa explained.

"It's not fair," I put in. "We didn't do anything wrong."

"Tell that to Mr. Bladvig," Louisa said.

"Hey!" I cried. "That's whose fault it is! Mr. Bladvig's!"

"Really." Louisa nodded. "If he hadn't come out of the music room and seen us petting Spike, we wouldn't even be in trouble."

"What about that redheaded kid?" I asked. "The one whose locker is next to Frankie's? What's his name—Jeff."

"Are you in *loooove* with Jeff?" Jimmy asked me.

4

I ignored him. "I bet Jeff is mad at Frankie," I went on.

"Why is Jeff mad at Frankie?" Jimmy asked.

"Jimmy, you don't even know Frankie and Jeff!" I exclaimed. "Why do you care?"

"Mr. Bladvig dragged Jeff off to Mr. Emerson's office with the rest of us, and he was just standing at his locker. He wasn't even looking at Spike," Louisa explained to him.

"I've got it!" I cried. "This is all *Spike's* fault."

Because of one stupid pet rat, I had to visit a kid I didn't even know.

One stupid white rat got us into all this trouble, I thought miserably.

Well, we'll go visit Max, and that will be the end of it, I told myself.

But I was wrong.

It was just the beginning.

The beginning of *real* trouble.

2

"**M**ax *would* live on Fear Street." Louisa shuddered as we walked down Hawthorne Drive. "Hey, there's Frankie!" She waved.

Frankie ran to catch up with us. It took him only a few strides—because everything about Frankie was long.

He had long, skinny legs. And long, thin arms— they practically hung down to his knees. He had a long, narrow face, with a long, straight nose. And long, stringy brown hair.

When he caught up to us, I noticed his T-shirt. It was long too. And blue—just like his eyes. It said DARE ME!

The three of us walked to Park Drive. Louisa

glanced over her shoulder. "Isn't that Jeff?" She pointed to a thin redheaded boy walking behind us. "Maybe we should wait for him."

As he walked up, I glanced at my watch. "Hey, guys, it's almost five," I warned. "We're going to be late!"

"We could cut through Mrs. Marder's yard," Frankie said.

"No way!" I cried. Didn't he know what people said about Mrs. Marder? "She's a witch!"

Louisa's dark eyes widened. "Right!" she agreed. "No way am I getting hexed!"

"You're afraid of *Mrs. Murder?*" Frankie said, chuckling. "I'm not."

"Well, you should be," I told him. "Don't you remember what happened to Gina Logan?"

"No, I don't," Jeff said. "What happened to her?"

"She went into Mrs. Marder's yard. And no one ever saw her again!"

"I heard Gina's family moved to Utah," Frankie pointed out.

"That's not what I heard." Louisa shook her head sadly. "She just disappeared!"

"Oh, sure," Jeff scoffed.

"No, really," Louisa insisted. "Mrs. Marder is weird. She has hundreds of cats—and they hiss

7

all the time. She hates kids. She's really scary."

"Scarier than double detention?" Frankie asked. "Because that's what Mr. Emerson said we'd get if we're late."

Frankie had a point. Two minutes of running through a witch's backyard was better than two weeks of detention.

"I don't think we should cut through," Jeff said suddenly.

"Don't tell me you're scared too!" Frankie teased.

"I'm not scared!" Jeff scowled. "I just don't think we should go through her yard, that's all. It's trespassing."

Trespassing? I glanced at Louisa and rolled my eyes. Who cared about that?

I studied Mrs. Marder's house. Its gray paint had peeled away. The bare wood underneath was splintered and rotted. A rickety porch ran all the way around the house.

I stared up at the windows. Dark, grimy windows behind crumbling, crooked shutters.

I turned and gazed across the street. Nothing there but a vacant lot with a huge hole in the ground. It looked as if someone had started to build a house and then gave up.

Who could blame them? Who would want to live across the street from *Mrs. Murder?*

I turned back to Mrs. Marder's house. Her yard was filled with cats. Cats everywhere. All black.

Black cats snoozing on the porch railing. Crouching on the windowsills. Stalking through the weedy grass.

"Max's house is right behind Mrs. Marder's," Frankie whispered. "Follow me on three. One . . . two . . . three!" He opened the creaky front gate and dashed around the side of her house.

Well, that settled that. Louisa, Jeff, and I sprinted after Frankie.

As I rounded the house, something caught my eye.

Mrs. Marder! Standing on the porch.

She held a stick in her bony hands. No, a broom! A green bandanna that was tied around her head only partly covered her coarse gray hair. I could see the deep wrinkles in her skin—and the evil glow in her dark green eyes.

"You rotten kids!" she screeched, shaking her broom at us.

I ran on. Past a wheelbarrow full of soil. Past an old stone birdbath with a face carved into its base.

No. Not a face.

A *skull!* A skull with hollow, staring eyes and a mouth opened wide in a silent scream!

"Come back here!" Mrs. Marder shrieked.

I ran faster—and tripped over a cat. It hissed—arching its back and baring its teeth. I fell on top of a tray of little flowerpots. Sent them shattering to the ground.

"My herbs!" Mrs. Marder shrieked. "You've ruined them! You've destroyed them all!"

My heart pounded as I scrambled to my feet.

Mrs. Marder pointed a bony finger at me. "You will pay!"

All the black cats gathered around her. They arched their backs. And hissed at me. Hissed horribly.

"I'll make you pay!" she yelled.

I dove behind a clump of bushes at the back of the yard—and found Louisa, Jeff, and Frankie hiding there.

"Wow! Brittany broke a few flowerpots, but Mrs. Marder went ballistic!" Frankie shook his head in disbelief. "Did you hear her?"

"She's going inside now," Jeff said. "Come on. Let's go."

"Not yet." Frankie darted out from the bushes. He ran for the wheelbarrow and kicked it over. Dark soil spilled out into the weeds.

10

The back door swung open.

Mrs. Marder burst outside. She raised her broom high in the air. She shook it angrily.

"You'll pay for this!" she screamed. "I'll make you pay! I'll make all of you pay!"

3

We ran from Mrs. Marder's yard as fast as we could.

I could hardly breathe by the time we got to Max's front door.

"You'll pay! You'll all pay!" Mrs. Marder's shrieks rang in my ears. My legs began to tremble.

My hand shook too as I rang Max's doorbell. I took a deep breath to steady myself.

I checked my watch. Oh, great. We ran through that horrible woman's yard—and we were late anyway.

I peered up at Max's house. It was a one-story brick house with freshly painted white shutters. Neat little bushes surrounded it. What a pretty house, I thought—the opposite of Mrs. Marder's scary house.

A pretty blond woman answered the door. "Hi!" she greeted us. "I'm Mrs. Davidson, Max's mom."

Mrs. Davidson had cheerful green eyes and a nice smile. Her long blond hair was held loosely in a silver clip. She wore an apple-green top, leggings, and high-top sneakers. Very cool.

She held the door open and we stepped inside.

"I'm Louisa Wong," Louisa said first.

"Jeff de Winter," Jeff mumbled.

"I'm Brittany Carson," I volunteered.

Frankie stepped up last. "Todaro," he announced, strutting through the door. "Frankie."

Mrs. Davidson invited us to sit down in the living room. "I told Mr. Emerson I'd call him when you arrived," she said. "And you're right on time! I'll go call now. Excuse me."

She walked into the kitchen. I heard her talking on the phone through the closed kitchen door. She was nice to say we'd made it on time!

"It's so kind of you to visit Max!" Mrs. Davidson exclaimed when she came back.

None of us mentioned that we didn't have much choice!

"We moved to Shadyside only last week," Mrs. Davidson went on. "Max hoped to start seventh grade next week. But—"

13

"We're in seventh grade too," Louisa interrupted.

"Well, maybe you can help him catch up when he gets back to school. Max's doctor said he has to stay in bed for three more weeks," Mrs. Davidson told us. "He's getting over pneumonia, so he has to rest."

Then she stood up. "Well, let's not keep Max waiting any longer. He's so excited about meeting you."

The four of us followed her down a long hallway.

At the end of the hallway a door stood halfway open. Mrs. Davidson pushed it open all the way. "Max?" she said. "Some students from Shadyside Middle School are here to meet you."

We stepped into Max's room. Windows stretched all along one wall. But they didn't let in much light.

A boy sat on a bed at one end of the shadowy room. He looked small for a seventh-grader. He wore white long-sleeved pajamas. He had pale skin. And pale blond hair. He even had pale blue eyes— but they were ringed with dark circles.

Poor kid, I thought. He does look sick!

"Hi, Max!" Louisa said cheerily.

Max nodded hello.

Then there was an awkward silence.

"So—you have a Monopoly board or anything?" Jeff asked Max.

14

Max shook his head no this time. He sure wasn't making this easy!

"Uh—would you like to talk? Or play a game?" I asked him.

"Cards," he said in a soft voice. He drew a deck from under his covers.

Cards? My heart sank. I just couldn't seem to get away from cards!

"Great," I lied, trying to make my voice cheerful.

"Go on over to the table, kids." Mrs. Davidson nodded to the end of the room opposite Max's bed.

Max stood up. He walked slowly to the table. "Let's play hearts," he suggested in a quiet voice.

"Good thinking, Max," Mrs. Davidson told him. "Five can play that. Do you kids know how?"

We all nodded as we sat down. Max shuffled the deck.

"Now Max will ask someone to cut the cards," Mrs. Davidson told us. "That's good card manners."

Max pushed the deck toward Frankie.

"Lift some cards from the top of the deck—as many as you want," Mrs. Davidson instructed. "Then put the cards from the bottom of the deck on top of them."

After Frankie cut the cards, Max began to deal. I noticed that he was a serious nail-biter. The tips of his fingers were all ragged and chewed.

"Wait to pick up your cards until they're all dealt," Mrs. Davidson told us. "That's good card manners too."

When Max finished dealing, we picked up our hands.

"Have fun, kids!" Mrs. Davidson said, and left the room.

I studied my cards one at a time. Two of clubs. Six of hearts. Three of diamonds. Jack of—

A horrible scream split the air!

I jumped.

Frankie dropped his cards to the floor.

"Frankie!" I exclaimed, startled. "What's wrong?"

Frankie stared, eyes wide open. His jaw dropped.

And he let out the most horrifying scream I'd ever heard.

4

The awful, piercing scream went on and on.

I clapped my hands to my ears. "Frankie!" I cried again. "What's wrong! Tell us—what's wrong!"

Frankie turned to me—and the screaming stopped. Stopped suddenly, as if a knife sliced it off mid-scream. But his mouth still hung open.

Mrs. Davidson ran into Max's room. "What happened?" she cried. "Is someone hurt? Who screamed?"

"Frankie did," Louisa told her.

"I did not!" Frankie protested.

We all stared at him. "Yes, you did!" Louisa exclaimed. "Your mouth was wide open. We all heard you. Screaming like a maniac."

"I wasn't screaming," Frankie said flatly.

"Yeah, right," I said. "You nearly burst my eardrums. You dropped all your cards—then you started screaming."

"I don't know what you mean about screaming." Frankie spoke slowly. "I know I dropped my cards. It was because of—because of the joker."

Frankie glanced under the table. We all followed his gaze.

There his cards lay—all facedown. All but one. All but the joker.

The joker—it was like no joker I had ever seen.

It had huge round eyes that bulged right out of their sockets. Hideous eyes! I felt as if they could *see* me!

Its bright red lips curved up in a crooked, evil smile.

The joker wore a floppy green cap with bells. In its hand it held a stick. On the top of the stick sat a skull. A skull with eyes that glowed like hot coals!

"Yuck!" Louisa squealed, turning her face away. "It's so ugly!"

I started to turn away too—when the joker's face began to move!

Its eyeballs darted left and right! First it peered at me. Then it glared at Louisa. Then Jeff.

The joker's eyeballs came to rest on Frankie. Its mouth twisted open—in a grin full of yellow, jagged teeth.

18

I stared in horror. I couldn't speak.

"What's wrong?" Max's mom asked. "What are you looking at?"

At the sound of her voice, the joker's ugly face froze.

Had it really moved?

Or had I imagined it?

I glanced at my friends. Had they seen it?

But they were all staring at *me*. "Brit, what's the matter?" Louisa asked. "You're so pale!"

"The joker . . ." I began. But then I trailed off. No way. It wasn't possible. I *couldn't* have seen it move!

Could I?

Mrs. Davidson bent and picked up the card. "What a horrible card!" she cried. She gathered up the other cards from the floor.

"Let me have all the cards, kids," she said. "I'll check to make sure there aren't any more jokers. How in the world did this terrible-looking thing get into the deck in the first place?"

Max only shrugged as he handed his mom his cards. He didn't seem very upset about the joker. Maybe his doctor told him not to get excited—about anything.

But I was plenty excited. My heart was racing!

"That was horrible," I told Frankie. "That wasn't a regular joker. No wonder you screamed."

"I told you—I didn't scream," Frankie said.

"Come on, Frankie," Jeff said. "Just admit it. We all heard you. I bet the whole neighborhood heard you."

Frankie glared. "Would you all just—"

"There. I've checked the deck. There aren't any more ugly jokers," Mrs. Davidson interrupted. She handed the deck of cards to Max. "Remember, it's good card manners to let someone cut the cards, Max."

Max began shuffling.

"Um . . . you really want to play?" I asked.

Max shrugged. "Why not?"

"Yes, but . . ." I began. I stopped. With the jokers out of the deck, I guess it was okay to play.

We played hand after hand of hearts. By the time the four of us left Max's house, I saw clubs and diamonds, hearts and spades swimming before my eyes.

And I still saw that ugly joker. Saw its evil grin. Saw it move.

How could a single card be so frightening?

How?

20

5

"I wish we'd left earlier," Louisa grumbled as we walked along Fear Street in the dark. "I hate this street at night."

"It seems like the streetlights are always broken here," I complained. "I can't see a thing!"

"We could always cut through Mrs. *Murder's* yard again," Frankie suggested.

"No way!" I said. Then I heard something. "Hey, listen. What's that?"

I glanced in the direction of Mrs. Marder's house. But it was too dark to see anything.

"I hear something rattling," Jeff whispered.

Rattling—that was the sound I heard. Rattling—like someone shaking a can full of pebbles.

"I hear it," Louisa agreed. "Listen. It's getting louder."

My eyes searched the shadows along Fear Street.

"Hey!" Frankie yelled suddenly. "Watch it, buddy!"

I whirled around.

I saw Frankie sprawled on the sidewalk. A small figure bent over him. A kid. He must have run into Frankie and knocked him down. Now he said something to Frankie.

"Frankie!" Louisa called. "Are you okay?"

Frankie didn't answer.

The figure straightened up. He wasn't very tall. He wore a green hat with a brim pulled down low over his forehead. I couldn't make out his face under the brim. The only thing I could see clearly was the stick he held in his hand.

I ran toward Frankie—and the shadowy figure shook his stick fiercely. Something rattled inside. He let out a scream—and raced away into the darkness.

"Frankie, are you okay?" I asked. "Who was that?"

"I don't know, some little kid," Frankie groaned. "Boy, he sure slammed into me hard!" He stood up and rubbed his arm.

The four of us huddled close together as we walked along Fear Street.

"He said something weird," Frankie began as we headed home. "It sounded like 'We shake the skull. . . .' No. That wasn't it."

He frowned, trying to remember. "I know. 'We shake the skull with eyes that gleam.'"

"That doesn't make any sense," Jeff said.

Frankie shrugged. "That's what it sounded like."

"That can't be what he said. Maybe he said something like, sorry to shake you up," Louisa suggested.

"No. That's not what he said." Frankie sounded definite.

That didn't stop Louisa. "Maybe the skull part was about how he hoped you didn't crack *your* skull."

Frankie groaned. "Louisa. Do me a favor. Stop guessing."

We didn't talk the rest of the way to Frankie's house. I had to admit, Louisa's explanations were pretty lame.

Frankie paused on his porch. "Listen," he said. "I'm sorry about getting you guys in trouble."

By the porch light I saw that Frankie was pretty scraped up. The side of his face was raw where he'd hit the pavement. And there was a strange, dark bruise above his wrist. It looked almost as if it were in the shape of a flower. Or something.

"Frankie, that bruise . . ." I pointed to his arm.

"It's shaped like . . . like a club," I said, suddenly seeing it.

"A club?" Frankie studied the bruise. "What do you mean?"

"You know—the card suit," I said. "Like spades, or hearts."

"Huh?" He stared at me.

"Brit, I think you're losing it," Louisa told me.

Maybe. But I wasn't so sure.

First—there was that hideous joker. Now—the club-shaped mark on Frankie's arm. Was I imagining them because I didn't like cards?

Or was there something going on?

Something bad?

6

"Truth or dare!" Louisa challenged me in the cafeteria on Monday. "Do you think Frankie is cute?"

"Spike is cute," I replied, reminding her of what she said about the rat. "Frankie is—interesting."

"He's cute," Louisa told me. "But he needs a haircut."

"You always want to fix everybody's hair!" I exclaimed.

I checked my watch. Oh, no—I was late! I bolted from my seat.

"Hey! Where are you going?" Louisa asked.

"I almost forgot! I have to meet Frankie," I explained. "Mr. Emerson wants us to hang a

25

community-service club poster. Lunch period is the only time we can do it."

"You and Frankie, huh?" Louisa waggled her eyebrows at me.

I rolled my eyes. "Louisa, quit it! Meet me by my locker after school, okay?" I gathered up my books.

"Right." Louisa nodded. "Tell Frankie I said hi!"

I charged out of the cafeteria. In the main hallway I spotted Frankie walking with the principal. Mr. Emerson had a large roll of poster paper under one arm. I hurried to meet them.

"Brittany." Mr. Emerson smiled. "I've been hearing about your visit with Max on Saturday. His mother said you really cheered him up. That's terrific! Maybe your visits will help him get well faster."

"I hope so," I said. And I did hope Max felt better. But I had another reason too. Between Max and my little brother, I was really sick of cards!

Mr. Emerson showed us where he wanted us to put up the poster. He handed me a roll of masking tape.

"Mr. Stock from maintenance set this up for you," he said, pointing to a five-rung ladder. "If the tape runs out, there's another roll on my desk. Help yourself." Then he left.

"Okay, let's see how high I can hang this baby." Frankie started up the ladder with the poster.

"I'll make tape rolls," I offered. "You can stick them under the edges of the poster. That way the tape won't show."

I began tearing off strips of masking tape and rolling them with the sticky side out.

When Frankie was on the fourth rung of the ladder, he reached down for a tape roll.

I handed it to him—and caught a glimpse of his arm.

"Frankie!" I exclaimed. "That bruise!"

The bruise had darkened. Its outline had become more definite. Now it looked *exactly* like a black three-leaf clover. Like a club.

"Yeah. It's weird." Frankie took the tape. "You know what else? It doesn't hurt. Bruises definitely hurt. And this one doesn't."

We both stared at the strange mark on Frankie's arm. "Maybe it's dirt," I said.

"That's what I thought," he replied. "But I tried scrubbing it. It won't come off."

If it isn't a bruise and it isn't dirt—what is it? I wondered as I made tape loops.

I came to the end of the roll. "Hey, Frankie. Don't move!" I ordered. "We're out of tape."

I hurried around the corner to the principal's office to get another roll. As I reached for the tape on his desk, I heard a humming sound. Had Mr. Emerson left his computer on?

I checked. No.

A fan? No.

I shrugged and left the office.

In the hallway I could still hear the sound. But it changed from a hum to a hiss.

Suddenly I pictured Mrs. Marder's hissing, snarling cats. What an odd thing to think about.

As I walked down the corridor, the sound grew louder.

Now it didn't sound so much like hissing—more like rattling.

Like the sound we heard last night on Fear Street.

I hurried down the hall.

The rattling grew louder.

I started to run.

"Frankie!" I called.

He didn't answer.

Then I heard a crash!

And a horrible scream!

"Frankie!" I shouted. "Are you okay? *Frankie!*"

7

I skidded around the corner. Then I screeched to a stop.

"Oh, no!" My knees began to tremble. "Frankie! How did this happen?"

Frankie lay on the floor.

The ladder rested on top of him.

The poster was draped over his body.

"Are you okay?" I shoved the ladder off him.

But Frankie didn't answer. He didn't move.

I ripped away pieces of the heavy poster. "Frankie! Say something!" I begged.

Frankie moaned. I breathed a sigh of relief.

"What happened?" I demanded as he sat up.

"I don't know." He shook his head. "It all

happened so fast." Then he lowered his voice. "But I didn't fall."

"What do you mean?"

"First I heard this sound. This—rattling sound," he said.

Frankie heard it too! So I didn't imagine it!

"Then," he went on, "these two kids came zooming down the hall. Little kids. Like second-graders. They pushed the ladder over. Then one of them said something—"

"Frankie," I interrupted. "The sound you heard—was it the same as that night on Fear Street? That rattling sound?"

"Yeah." Frankie nodded. "It *was* the same."

He stared off into space for a second.

I waved a hand in front of his face. "Can you remember anything about the kids who pushed over the ladder?" I asked him. "What they said? What they looked like?"

"They sped down the hall so fast," Frankie told me, "and—wait a sec. There *is* one thing. They had on strange hats."

I don't know why, but my mind suddenly flashed on Mrs. Marder again. Mrs. Marder—with the green bandanna tied around her head. Mrs. Marder—screaming at us. Screaming about how she would make us pay.

30

"Well." Frankie shrugged. "I guess I'm okay anyway."

We cleaned up the mess on the floor. Later we'd have to explain to Mr. Emerson what happened to the poster.

As we walked to our next class, Frankie still seemed sort of dazed. He had this distant look in his eyes, like he was trying really hard to remember something.

He turned to me. "One of the kids who knocked over the ladder said, 'We make our marks, we laugh and scream!' " he told me. "Weird, huh?"

I drew in a breath. It *was* weird. "What about last night on Fear Street? What did you think that kid said?"

" 'We shake the skull with eyes that gleam,' " Frankie remembered.

"Hey!" I cried. "It's some kind of rhyme. Listen. 'We shake the skull with eyes that gleam! We make our marks, we laugh and scream!' See? The lines go together."

A bell rang. Kids poured out of classrooms into the hallway. They pushed by us. But Frankie and I stood there, staring at each other.

"Something very weird is going on," I said at last.

Frankie raised his hand and touched the bump on his forehead.

When I saw his arm, I gasped.

"What's the matter?" Frankie asked. "What's wrong?"

I opened my mouth. But no words came out.

"Stop it, Brit!" Frankie cried. "Say something!"

All I could do was point to his arm.

There was another mark on it.

Above the club.

But this one wasn't black.

It was red.

And it was in a shape I knew.

The shape of a perfect diamond.

8

"It—it looks like a diamond," Frankie whispered. His eyes were glued to the mysterious shape on his arm.

I rubbed my finger over the club and the diamond. They were smooth. "They're like tattoos."

"They *are* like tattoos," he agreed. "But I haven't been to any tattoo places. So how did I get them?"

Neither of us knew.

That afternoon the four of us headed for Max's house again.

I kept waiting for Frankie to tell Louisa and Jeff about getting pushed off the ladder. Or about the diamond-shaped mark on his arm. But he just

33

walked along silently. Maybe he was trying to forget.

"What are we going to do with Max today?" Louisa asked.

"Let's think of something new," I suggested. "Something besides card games."

"What else can we play with a sick kid?" Jeff asked. "Touch football?"

"No," I snapped. "But what about Monopoly? Or Scrabble? I'd even play Candy Land! Anything but cards."

"Oh, Brittany," Jeff said. "It's only for a couple of hours."

I glanced at Frankie. Why didn't he speak up? Why didn't he tell anyone about the marks on his arm? I wondered. He had even more reason than I did for being sick of cards.

Well, he could keep quiet if he wanted to. I was going to say something.

"Frankie?" I asked. "Are those marks still on your arm?"

"What marks?" Louisa asked.

Frankie pulled up his shirt cuff. They were there all right.

"Do you see them, Louisa?" I asked her. "A club shape and a diamond?"

Louisa squinted. "Yeah, I guess I see what you mean," she admitted. "I can sort of see the shapes."

"You guys are crazy," Jeff declared. "One's a dark bruise and the other's a reddish scrape. That's all."

"Right," Frankie agreed, pulling down his cuff in a rush. "That's all. No big deal."

I stared at him. I didn't know what to say.

Those marks on his arm were definitely a club and a diamond.

Frankie *knew* they were strange. That they weren't a bruise and a scrape. That each one had come after someone pushed him down. We had talked about it! Why was he denying it now?

We turned the corner. There was Mrs. Marder's witchy old house.

I shivered as I thought about her yelling at me.

What did she mean, she was going to make us pay?

We stopped at the gate and stared into her yard. No sign of her. She was probably in her kitchen, brewing up some strange potion!

But her cats stalked everywhere. Under the bushes. Through the grass. Around the birdbath— hungrily eyeing the sparrows splashing in it.

"We should do something to help those poor little birdies," Frankie said suddenly. His voice had a nasty edge. "Come on!" He opened the gate and darted into the yard.

Jeff groaned.

Frankie stopped and turned toward us. A wicked grin crossed his face. He waved us in.

"What do you think, Brit?" Louisa whispered. "Should we go?"

"I don't know," I answered, biting my lip. "Mrs. Marder is really mad at us already."

"I'm not going," Jeff declared. "I'm taking the long way to Max's. See you." He turned and walked toward Fear Street.

Frankie vanished around the side of Mrs. Marder's house.

"Brit, we have to get Frankie out of there," Louisa whispered. "Before *Mrs. Murder* sees him!"

"Right." I grabbed her arm. "Let's go!"

We ran through the gate.

My heart pounded as we dashed across the yard. Black cats hissed at us as they scattered.

I spotted Frankie. He stood over some big pots filled with blooming geranium plants. As I watched, he lifted up the biggest plant and ran with it across the yard.

"Frankie!" I called in a hoarse whisper. "What are you doing?"

He didn't answer. He kept running. Then he heaved the pot—flowers and all—right into the middle of the birdbath. It made an awful crash.

"There!" he cried loudly. "That'll keep the birdies out of danger!"

I groaned. Why did he do *that?*

"Are you nuts?" Louisa shouted at Frankie. "Come on, Brit! Let's get out of here!"

"Too bad, kitties!" Frankie yelled. "No birdies for you! Fly away birds. Fly away." He ran around the yard, flapping his arms. "You're safe now."

"You're not!" a voice screamed behind us.

I gave a yelp of surprise.

I whipped my head around.

Mrs. Marder!

"I warned you!" she shrieked. "Now you'll pay!"

9

Mrs. Marder took a step toward us. The green bandanna on her head fluttered in the wind.

"You!" she screamed.

Was she pointing at me?

"Run!" I cried. "Let's get out of here!"

Louisa, Frankie, and I charged out of the yard. We didn't stop running until we reached Max's house.

I put out my hands and stopped myself on a tree trunk, gasping for breath.

"Did you see the awful look in her eyes?" I cried.

"I did." Louisa's voice shook. "I'm scared, Brit! Maybe we should tell Mrs. Davidson what happened."

Jeff stood on the front steps, looking smug. When he saw us, he turned and rang the bell.

Mrs. Davidson opened the door wearing a jade-green T-shirt and dark jeans. "Hi, kids!" she greeted us. "Come in! Max can't wait to get started today. He has the cards all shuffled."

"Mrs. Davidson, we have to talk to you," Louisa declared.

"Of course." A look of concern came over Mrs. Davidson's face. "Is something wrong?"

"You know the house right behind yours?" Louisa asked as we entered the living room.

Mrs. Davidson nodded. "The Marder house."

"Mrs. Marder is evil!" I blurted out. "She's a witch!"

"Oh, that poor woman!" Mrs. Davidson said. "She isn't evil! She doesn't take much time with her appearance, that's all."

"But all those stories about her—" I began.

Mrs. Davidson shook her head. "You mustn't believe those stories. They are so silly! Especially the one about the kids who trespassed in her yard."

"What kids?" Louisa asked. "I never heard that story."

"Oh, it's nothing. Just a ridiculous rumor." Mrs. Davidson frowned slightly. "I shouldn't repeat it. These kinds of rumors are so mean."

"Please tell us," I begged. "Please!"

"Oh, all right." Mrs. Davidson sighed. "But remember—it's just a story. A silly story."

I wasn't so sure about that. Not at all.

"One day," Mrs. Davidson began, "four children supposedly wandered into Mrs. Marder's backyard. They were only seven or eight years old. Too young to know any better. They stepped on one of her plants or something. When she saw what they'd done—so the story goes—she got really angry and put a spell on them."

"A spell?" My heart was racing. "What kind of spell?"

"Oh, it's too silly to tell." Mrs. Davidson started to leave the room. "Let's go see Max."

"No!" I yelled. "I mean, please tell us the rest of the story. Please."

Mrs. Davidson's glance moved across each of our faces. "Oh, all right. I suppose everyone likes a scary story now and then. But remember—it's just a story."

We all nodded, eager to hear the rest. And dreading it at the same time.

"She chased the children out of her yard," Mrs. Davidson went on. "But from that moment on, the children complained that little creatures followed them everywhere. Attacking them when they least expected it."

40

Blood drained from Frankie's face. He looked scared to death.

I gasped.

"Oh, kids! It's only a silly story." Mrs. Davidson shook her head. "You don't have anything to worry about."

"Yes, we do!" Louisa cried. "We ran through her garden. And Frankie dumped over her wheelbarrow and smashed a big plant in her birdbath!"

I glanced at Frankie. Now he had a strange grin on his face.

"I told you—it was just a silly story," Mrs. Davidson said soothingly. "Nothing bad is going to happen to you."

We stared silently at Mrs. Davidson. We all looked pretty scared. All except Jeff. He still looked smug. Like he wanted to say "I told you so."

"Listen." Mrs. Davidson broke the silence. "Why don't I phone Mrs. Marder and tell her you're very sorry for ruining her plant? I'll tell her how nice you've been to Max. She won't stay mad long."

"Oh, would you?" I cried with relief.

"I'll do it right now." Mrs. Davidson stood up and went into the kitchen, closing the door behind her.

Soon I heard her talking. I couldn't make out what she was saying. But the sound of her voice on the phone made me feel better.

41

Mrs. Davidson returned, smiling. "I told Mrs. Marder you didn't mean any harm," she reported. "And I told her how much your visits have helped Max."

"Is—is she still angry at us?" I stammered.

"Well, yes," Mrs. Davidson admitted. "But don't worry. She'll calm down. I offered to pay for the plant—but she said no. Then I promised her that you wouldn't do anything like this again. Now, run on down the hall. Max is waiting!"

I followed my friends to Max's room, thankful that Mrs. Davidson had called Mrs. Marder. Even though Mrs. Marder was still angry, I felt a little better. At least she knew we were sorry.

Max sat at the table shuffling the cards. When we walked into his room, he glanced up. The circles under his eyes seemed darker than ever.

"Hi, Max!" I slid into a chair next to his. I leaned toward him. "Listen," I whispered, "you think we could play something besides cards today?"

Max stared at me with his pale blue eyes. Then he shook his head. "No. Let's play cards," he said. "That's why you're here."

"We're not here to play cards, Max. We're here to visit you because you're sick," I told him. "Can't we play something else? I don't really like cards."

A smile appeared on Max's lips. But he only

42

shoved the cards toward me so I could cut them.

As he began dealing, I thought I heard him whisper, "I don't either." But when I glanced over at him, he was staring straight ahead, dealing.

We didn't pick up our cards until they were all dealt. Mrs. Davidson said that was good card manners.

I opened my hand one card at a time. I'd looked at about half of my cards, when I heard it.

A piercing scream.

So loud, I dropped my cards and covered my ears.

The scream went on and on, louder and louder.

And then it stopped. Suddenly.

Now all I could hear was Louisa.

"No!" she was yelling. "Get it away!"

She flung a card out of her hand.

It landed on the table, faceup.

We all stared at it.

It was the face of another hideous joker! But this one was different from the one Frankie had been dealt. This one had green skin and small, bloodshot eyes. Its mouth turned down in a frown.

It wore the same green hat with bells at the tip. And it held the same stick—a skull at the top, with awful, gleaming eyes!

I couldn't take my eyes off the joker's hideous face.

As I stared at it—the mouth suddenly began to move!

The joker's frown widened into a cruel snarl. The joker's little eyes twirled around and around in their sockets.

And the joker opened its mouth in another horrifying wail.

10

~~~~~~~

Mrs. Davidson burst into Max's room.

"What's the matter?" she cried. "Who screamed?"

"It was this!" Louisa wailed. She pointed to the card.

"The joker?" Mrs. Davidson gasped. "You mean the *card* screamed?"

Louisa nodded.

"Nonsense!" Mrs. Davidson exclaimed. "You know that's impossible. You're all upset because the card is so ugly."

She slipped the card in her pocket. Then she reached for the deck. "I don't know how it got in there. I thought I took all the jokers out myself. Sorry, I guess I missed this one."

I peered over Mrs. Davidson's shoulder as she studied the cards one by one. "Okay, no more jokers. They're all gone." She smiled and handed the deck back to Max.

"I don't want to play anymore," Louisa said the minute Mrs. Davidson left the room. "Max—please. Let's play something else."

Max ignored her. He shuffled a few times. He asked Jeff to cut, and then he dealt. We picked up our cards. We didn't know what else to do.

Instantly, the screaming began!

"Get it away!" Louisa cried. She threw her cards down on the table and leapt from her chair. "It's here!" she shrieked. "It's *screaming!*"

There it was!

On the table.

The joker!

And it was screaming!

I gaped at the joker's awful face. Stared at its horrible mouth as it let out its hideous scream.

How could this be? How did it get back in the deck?

How could it scream?

How could a card scream?

Suddenly, it fell silent again.

My eyes darted from Louisa, to Jeff, to Frankie.

Louisa and Jeff stared at the card in horror.

Frankie's glance was cool, almost amused.

Then I heard the sound.

Hssssssss!

I glanced toward the window.

A black cat crouched on the sill outside Max's window!

It shifted its gaze—until its eyes rested on me. Its evil, gleaming green eyes.

That was when it hit me.

"It's Mrs. Marder!" I cried, tossing my cards down. "She's the one making these jokers appear. *She's* the one making them scream!"

Everyone stared at me.

Then Frankie started laughing like a maniac.

"It's not funny!" I yelled at him. "It's true. One of her cats is here right now! Look!" I pointed to the windowsill.

But the cat had vanished.

"It was there!" I insisted. "Didn't any of you see it?"

Jeff, Louisa, and Max shook their heads.

Frankie started laughing again.

"I *know* Mrs. Marder's behind this somehow," I declared.

"Oh, dear." Mrs. Davidson entered the room and scooped up the joker from the table. "Two cards must have been stuck together," she said softly.

She turned to Louisa. "Did you scream, dear? Did you scream at this ugly, ugly card?" Mrs. Davidson stared at the card in her hands and shuddered. "I can't blame you."

"I—I wasn't screaming," Louisa stammered. "It *was* the card. The card was screaming!"

"What imaginations you kids have!" Mrs. Davidson smiled. Shook her head. Then she left the room.

"You heard it!" Louisa exclaimed. "You heard it screaming. Didn't you?" She turned to Frankie and Jeff.

"Yeah, right," Jeff laughed. "Screaming card. Good one, Louisa."

Frankie's face was uncertain. "It doesn't make sense, but . . ." he began. Then he trailed off.

"Max?" Louisa asked. "You heard it. Right?"

"I heard the screaming," Max said evenly. "I heard you screaming."

But Louisa didn't scream.

I was sure of it.

It was the joker—and Mrs. Marder's evil magic made it happen. Now I was sure of *that* too.

Somehow—some way—I had to prove it.

"Thanks for coming home with me, Brit," Louisa said after we left Max's. We were in her kitchen,

48

hunting for something to eat. "My mom's meeting won't be over until eight," she went on. "I couldn't stand coming into a dark, empty house tonight. Not after what happened today."

I told Louisa all about Frankie falling off the ladder, and how he got the diamond-shaped mark on his arm. "What are we going to do?" I asked her now. "Mrs. Marder is behind all of this. I know it."

The color drained from Louisa's face. "I don't want to talk about it anymore," she said. "It's too creepy. Let's look at my new *Seventeen* magazine instead."

Louisa ran upstairs to her room to get the magazine.

I peeled the foil off the top of a container of yogurt. I took a spoonful—and froze.

Hsssss!

I listened closely.

Hsssss!

There it was again.

Coming from upstairs.

Growing louder.

I jumped up and ran for the steps.

The hissing turned to rattling. Loud rattling.

"Louisa!" I cried.

Louisa answered—with a terrified scream!

I bolted to the staircase.

Started to run up the steps.

49

But Louisa was rolling down them—headfirst.

"Louisa!" I shrieked as she tumbled into me.

Dizzy, I struggled to sit up—and saw the three short figures. Dressed all in black, except for their green hats.

They zoomed down the steps. Leapt over us. Flung open the front door.

And ran out into the night.

"Ohhhh!" Louisa moaned. "I—I hurt my ankle."

I helped her up. She hobbled into the family room and collapsed on the couch.

I ran to the front door and slammed it shut. I made *sure* it was locked.

"Those things—they appeared out of nowhere. Suddenly they were there—right next to me!"

"I—I saw them too." My voice shook.

"They lunged at me. They pushed me down the steps!" Louisa exclaimed.

"It's Mrs. Marder," I whispered. "It's Mrs. Marder's magic. Just like in the story Mrs. Davidson told us. It's just like what happened to those little kids! This is horrible!"

"It's worse than horrible," Louisa wailed. "One of those—those *things* said something to me."

"What? Louisa, what did it say?" I asked.

Louisa closed her eyes. Then she repeated what she had heard. " 'Her army strengthens day by day.' That's it."

Her army strengthens day by day. I repeated the words in my mind. What did it mean?

"Brittany, I'm scared!" Louisa hid her face in her hands.

I gasped.

"Louisa! Your arm!"

Louisa stared down at her left arm. "No!" she screamed. "No!"

On her arm was a bruise. A bruise in the shape of a black club.

She began rubbing it furiously, trying to make the mark disappear. But the club stayed—as if permanently printed on her skin.

I ran into the kitchen for a pencil and piece of paper. I wrote down what Frankie's attackers had said to him. Then I wrote down what Louisa had heard.

"Listen to this," I told Louisa. I read:

"We shake the skull with eyes that gleam
We make our marks, we laugh and scream
Her army strengthens day by day

52

"It's part of the rhyme!" I decided.

Louisa shrugged. "I don't get what it means."

"Me either," I confessed. "But it must mean something!"

I stared down at what I had written. "Let's see— the skull. There's a skull in the base of Mrs. Marder's birdbath. Did you see it?"

Louisa shook her head.

"Well, it's there. Maybe at night its eyes gleam."

"Wait." Louisa gazed off into the distance. Trying to remember something. "The joker card. It had a stick—and on top was a *skull!*"

"That's right!" I snapped my fingers. "And the skull had weird, glowing eyes!"

Now we were getting somewhere!

I read the next line. *"We make our marks. We laugh and scream.* The marks—they must be the club and diamond shapes," I said.

The pieces of the puzzle were starting to come together.

"The first time we went to Max's, Frankie was dealt a joker," I murmured, thinking back. "Then, on the way home, we heard hissing and rattling— and a scream. Then someone pushed Frankie down. After that we saw the club shape on his arm."

Louisa nodded.

53

"Today *you* were dealt the joker," I went on. "Then we heard hissing and rattling and a scream—and *you* were pushed down."

"But why?" Louisa whispered. "Why is it happening to us?"

"Mrs. Marder is doing this! She put a spell on us!" I exclaimed. "She said she'd make us pay for ruining her plants! She's evil. She's really evil!"

Louisa's face twisted as if she were about to cry. "What are we going to do?"

"We have to stop her," I declared.

"How?" Louisa demanded.

"I don't know," I admitted. "But I'm going to come up with a plan."

Louisa's mom came home then. I left a few minutes later.

I live just a few houses away from Louisa. I started for my house—in the dark. It's woodsy at Louisa's end of the street. The houses are spread out among the trees.

As I hurried home, something moving in the woods caught my eye.

I heard rustling.

And a high-pitched wail.

Terrified, I glanced over my shoulder.

Something shifted behind a bush. Something green!

And then I saw it—the top of a green hat.

As I stared in horror, the green hat rose. Up from behind the bushes.

No—not a green hat.

A green bandanna—on the head of Mrs. Marder!

She stared at me with the strangest smile on her face.

A completely evil smile.

12

"I'm so happy it's Saturday!" I sang as I passed the basketball to Jeff. "No cards at Max's house today!"

We were playing hoops in my driveway. Louisa and Frankie against me and Jeff. Jeff shot the ball back to me.

"Let's take a break," Louisa suggested. "My ankle's starting to hurt."

We sat down at the picnic table by our driveway. Our house is at the top of a high, steep hill. For a minute we all gazed down at the view of Shadyside.

"Only three more days of visiting Max," I said at last.

Jeff glanced at me. "Max is nice. Why don't you like him?"

"I like him fine," I protested. "I just don't want to play cards anymore!"

I hesitated a minute. Then I said what was really on my mind. Ever since I saw Mrs. Marder in the woods, I had been thinking of a plan. Now was my chance to spring it on everybody.

"I think we have to sneak into Mrs. Marder's house and find proof that she's behind the jokers!" I announced.

Jeff shook his head. "Mrs. Marder wouldn't hurt anybody."

His attitude was really starting to bug me. "How do you know, Jeff?" I demanded. I crossed my arms. "Why are you sticking up for Mrs. Marder? Do you know something we don't know?"

Jeff scowled. He picked up the basketball and angrily hurled it at the basket—hard! The ball bounded off the backboard and sailed out of our driveway.

"I'll get it!" Frankie jumped up and dashed down the hill. He ran until we couldn't see him anymore.

"Sorry," Jeff muttered. He sat back on the bench and scowled down at his feet. "Look," he began. "If you want to know—"

"Shhh!" Louisa interrupted him. "Listen!"

That's when I heard it.

Hsssss.

I sprang to my feet. "The hissing!"

57

I whirled around. Searching frantically for a black cat—or a little kid wearing a green hat.

I didn't see either one.

Then it hit me.

"Frankie!" I cried.

I raced down the hill. Jeff followed right behind me.

The hissing grew stronger.

Then the rattling sounds began.

At the bottom of the hill, four little kids on bicycles appeared from a side street.

Four little kids. Dressed all in black. Wearing green floppy hats.

Those hats . . .

Finally, I put it together.

They're not little kids at all, I realized in horror.

"What are those kids doing down there?" Jeff asked.

"Those aren't kids!" I cried, putting on more speed. "Don't you see? They're jokers! The jokers from the card deck!"

My sneakers pounded the grass as I ran down the hill.

I cupped my hands around my mouth. I tried to warn Frankie. "Look out!" I cried. But Frankie was chasing the ball at the bottom of the hill.

He didn't hear me.

He didn't see the jokers aiming straight for him.

The hissing and rattling grew louder.

Frankie bent down to pick up the ball.

A deep rumbling sound filled the air. Was it coming from the jokers?

No! It was a huge truck speeding up the road.

The jokers heard it too. They pedaled harder—and barreled right into Frankie.

The jolt knocked Frankie into the air. He landed in the street. And didn't move.

The truck driver should have hit the brakes. But he didn't.

The truck picked up speed.

"Noooo!" I screamed.

The truck headed straight for Frankie—and Frankie didn't move!

13

I froze.

Stared in horror as the truck aimed for Frankie.

Suddenly the truck's brakes began to squeal.

The driver saw Frankie! He was trying to stop the enormous truck!

The tires screamed as they skidded across the road—and the truck screeched to a stop. Barely a foot in front of Frankie.

The driver threw open his door and ran over to Frankie. Jeff and I reached him at the same time. We all knelt down by his side.

Frankie was knocked out cold. But he was breathing.

"What happened?" the driver asked. He was a big, muscular guy.

"A bike hit him," Jeff explained.

Frankie opened his eyes then. He groaned and sat up.

"Boy, that was a close one." The driver shook his head.

Frankie wouldn't let anyone call an ambulance. When the truck driver was sure Frankie was really okay, he left.

Jeff and I helped Frankie up. We walked him over to the sidewalk as Louisa came limping down the hill.

"What happened?" she cried.

"The jokers attacked Frankie again!" I told her. "Then he almost got run over by a truck!"

"Frankie, your arm!" Louisa covered her mouth with her hand.

We all stared at his left arm—and gasped.

Next to the club and diamond—there was something new.

A spade.

I whirled to face Jeff. *"Now* do you see them?" I shouted.

Jeff didn't answer. But his eyes were wide. Frightened.

"All I'm missing is a heart." Frankie's voice was very quiet. He ran his finger over the spade.

"Did the jokers say anything to you?" I asked him.

"Uh-huh." Frankie nodded. "'You play her game, she'll make you pay.'"

I grabbed Louisa's arm. "See? It is Mrs. Marder! That's what she said! She's making us pay by scaring us half to death! Listen to this:

"We shake the skull with eyes that gleam
We make our marks, we laugh and scream
Her army strengthens day by day
You play her game! She'll make you pay!

"Don't you guys see? The jokers are part of Mrs. Marder's spell!" I cried. "They must be part of her army. And they keep coming after us. More jokers each time. It started with one. But this time there were four. Next time there'll be *five!* We have to stop Mrs. Marder!"

"Hold on," Jeff protested. "You've got it all wrong, Brittany. I was trying to tell you before. I *know* Mrs. Marder."

My mouth fell open. "You *do?*" I managed to get out at last. "How come you never said anything?"

Jeff shrugged. "I deliver her groceries sometimes. That's all. I don't know her very well. But well enough to know that the stories aren't true. She's pretty cranky. But she isn't a witch. And I don't believe she's behind these joker attacks."

I stared at Jeff for a moment. How come he never told us before about knowing Mrs. Marder?

And another thing. How come he didn't run through Mrs. Marder's yard with the rest of us? And how come he took so long to admit that the marks on Frankie's arm were card suits?

Was he on our side? Or was he on Mrs. Marder's side?

I wasn't sure what to believe. But his grocery-delivery story gave me an idea.

"Maybe Mrs. Marder is behind the jokers," I said slowly, "and maybe she isn't. But we're going to find out."

"How?" Louisa asked.

"Simple," I answered. "We need to spy on Mrs. Marder."

14

"Okay, here's what we do," I said. "Jeff, you deliver a load of groceries to Mrs. Marder on Monday after school. While you're keeping her busy, we'll sneak around her house. See if we can find out anything about the jokers."

"One problem," Jeff said. "I just made a delivery to her house yesterday."

I still wasn't sure about Jeff. If he went along with our spy plan, then I'd know he was on our side—if not, he was definitely on Mrs. Marder's.

"So when she comes to the door, act confused," I told him. "Say there's been a mistake. Say anything! Just keep her busy. That way the rest of us can sneak onto her porch. We can peek in the windows. And maybe even slip inside for a fast look."

Jeff sighed. "This is a really stupid idea. But I'll do it. Only to prove how wrong you are about Mrs. Marder."

On Monday I met everyone at the grocery store before we went to Max's—*and* Mrs. Marder's house.

We all chipped in for the groceries. Then we headed for her house.

"Ready, Jeff?" I asked as we stood outside the front gate.

Jeff nodded. He shifted the grocery bag to his other arm. Then he opened the gate and started up the walk.

Three cats jumped down from a windowsill. They circled Jeff, rubbing against his legs.

Louisa, Frankie, and I walked on past the gate. We hid behind the bushes on the far side of the house. I peeked out at Jeff. He had his finger on the doorbell.

I kept my eyes glued to Jeff. He rang the bell again.

At last he turned and mouthed to us: "She's not home."

I hadn't thought of this. Mrs. Marder had always been home when we walked by.

"Okay," I said. "She's not home." I took a deep breath. "Let's see if we can sneak inside."

"I don't want to," Louisa protested. "What if she catches us? It's too scary."

"Come on!" Frankie suddenly leapt up from our hiding place. "Let's go!"

He raced through the gate, whooping. Then ran up the walk and galloped around on her porch.

"What is with him? He's acting like an idiot!" I whispered to Louisa as I dragged her through the front gate.

The cats in the yard hissed as we hurried to the back door. I turned the doorknob. *Click!*

Yes! It wasn't locked!

We crept inside.

Jeff quietly shut the door behind us. He set the bag of groceries down on the kitchen table.

Mrs. Marder's kitchen was dark. It had a musty smell. The floor was yellowed. Dirty dishes sat in the sink. A head of wilted lettuce lay on the kitchen table. Beside it—a sharp carving knife.

My heart beat wildly.

We were inside the evil woman's house!

Even in the dark, I could see the cats.

Cats sitting on the counters. Cats curled up on the floor. Cats stretched out on the kitchen chairs.

Black cats—everywhere.

"I can't do this!" Louisa whispered.

"Stay calm!" I told her, trying not to panic myself. "We'll be out of here in a few minutes. Okay, quick! Let's look around. Let's find out everything we can—and get out!"

While Frankie and Jeff poked around the kitchen, Louisa and I made our way down a dim hallway. The doors along it were all closed. Cats followed us, winding in and out among our feet.

I stopped before a door and cracked it open. Only a bathroom.

We walked to the next door.

"What if it's her bedroom?" Louisa whispered. "What if she's in there?"

Louisa's panic was catching. I could hardly hear her over my pounding heart.

I had to force myself to take hold of the old glass knob and twist.

I started to push open the door.

But all of a sudden Frankie and Jeff appeared. Frankie shoved me aside. He raced into the room ahead of me, laughing wildly.

"Frankie! What's wrong with—" I began.

I broke off.

We'd found Mrs. Marder's bedroom.

A big four-poster bed stood against one wall. Facing it I saw a chest of drawers. Set in another wall was a big window. And then . . .

Whoa!

An enormous telescope stood by the window!

I stepped into the room.

It was filled with even more black cats. They sat on the floor, glaring at us with glowing yellow eyes.

Frankie peered through the telescope. He turned to me, grinning. "Take a look!" he crowed.

I put my eye to the telescope—and gasped. "I don't believe it!"

15

I saw part of a room.

Max's room!

The telescope was aimed right at Max's window!

I backed away, speechless.

Louisa took a turn at the telescope. Her eyes were wide when she moved her head away from it.

Now it was Jeff's turn. He bent down to take a look. Then he stared at me.

"Maybe you're right, Brittany," he whispered. "Maybe Mrs. Marder does have something to do with the jokers."

"Of course I'm right!" I exclaimed. "She's been

69

spying on us. Watching us play cards. That's why she used jokers for her evil spell!"

"What are we going to do?" Louisa asked.

"We have our proof," I began. "Now—"

But that's as far as I got.

Suddenly the cats raced out the bedroom door. All at once. As if they had been called.

"She's home!" Louisa's voice squeaked. "We're trapped!"

"Come on!" Jeff whispered. He tiptoed quickly out of the bedroom. We followed right behind him.

Mrs. Marder's voice floated down the hallway to us. We could hear her talking to her cats.

"She's at the front door," Jeff whispered.

He led the way silently to the kitchen. To the back door.

He turned the knob.

I didn't hear any click.

He turned it again.

Nothing.

He began pulling on the door—hard!

But the door didn't open.

It was locked!

Cats started streaming into the kitchen. Howling madly.

70

"What's wrong, my little pets?" Mrs. Marder asked.

Oh, no! She's coming. She's right behind them!

Jeff pulled on the door with all his strength.

It wouldn't budge.

16

~~~

I grabbed the doorknob.

I yanked on it frantically. No use. The door was stuck tight.

"Do something!" Louisa whimpered. "She's coming!"

Frankie leapt to the door. He was grinning an awful grin.

He shoved Jeff and me aside and grabbed the doorknob. The door swung open.

How did he do that? I wondered. But I wasn't about to stop and ask. The four of us charged through the door at the same time!

We ran for our lives.

We raced through Mrs. Marder's backyard to

Max's. I didn't dare look over my shoulder. What if she was behind us? Chasing us?

Jeff rang the doorbell again and again—until Mrs. Davidson opened it.

"Mrs. Davidson!" Louisa cried as she rushed in. "Help!"

"What's the matter?" Mrs. Davidson asked. "Why are you all out of breath?"

"It's too hard to explain," Jeff told her once we were safely inside. "But we can't play cards with Max anymore."

Mrs. Davidson's eyes grew wide. "Why not?" she asked. "Your card games are doing Max a world of good!"

"Because when we play, Mrs. Marder spies on us!" I exclaimed. "With a telescope! Then she makes those awful jokers appear."

Mrs. Davidson raised her eyebrows.

"It's true," I insisted. "And they aren't only on the cards. They show up in real life too! They attacked Frankie and Louisa—just like the creatures who attacked those poor kids in the story you told us!"

Mrs. Davidson shook her head. "You're imagining this, Brittany dear." She patted me lightly on the shoulder.

My heart sank. Mrs. Davidson didn't believe us.

73

Probably no one would believe us, I realized with dread.

Who could believe such a wild story? As my words spilled out, even *I* thought I sounded crazy!

"Maybe you should play checkers today," Mrs. Davidson suggested.

"Could we play in the living room?" Jeff asked.

Mrs. Davidson looked puzzled. "Why?"

"It's the windows," Louisa told her. "Mrs. Marder spies on us through Max's windows."

"Oh, all right." Mrs. Davidson laughed. "The things you kids think up!" She led the way to Max's room.

"Max?" She bent over him. "Do you feel up to playing in the living room today?"

Max shook his head silently.

I glanced at the windows. They had shades rolled all the way up. "Let's pull down the shades," I suggested. "Then we can play in here."

Mrs. Davidson laughed again. But she lowered the shades. That made the room so dark, we had to turn on some lamps. But at least Mrs. Marder couldn't spy on us.

"Surprise, Max!" Louisa announced as she carried a checkerboard over to his bed. "We're going to play checkers. I'll play you first."

"And I'll play the winner," Jeff told Max.

But Max only stared at the checkerboard.

"What's the matter, Max?" Mrs. Davidson asked. "Wouldn't you like to play checkers for a change?"

Max shook his head. "No," he whispered.

He looked so unhappy.

"All right, Max." I sighed. "We'll play Hearts if you want."

"What?" Louisa exclaimed. "Am I hearing you right?"

"Yeah," Jeff added. "This is a switch for you."

I shrugged.

I had come prepared.

I reached into the back pocket of my jeans and drew out a deck of cards.

"There's no way Mrs. Marder could have put any evil spell on these," I announced as I handed my cards to Max. "Want to deal?"

Max smiled as he took the cards.

"Oh, thank you, kids!" Mrs. Davidson exclaimed. "Now everyone's happy. Have a good time!" Then she left us to our game.

Max slid out of bed. He walked slowly over to the table and sat down. He began to shuffle the deck. Louisa cut the cards and Max dealt our hands.

I didn't feel at all scared. I wasn't one bit worried about anybody getting a joker.

When the cards had all been dealt, I picked up my hand. I straightened the cards. I looked at the first one.

And gasped.

There it was—a hideous joker.

My hands began to tremble.

How could this be? How did the joker get into *my* deck?

17

I felt a weird buzzing in my ears. For a moment, everything in the room seemed to fade. To turn gray.

I shook my head.

Everything came back into focus. I was staring at the card in my hand. A joker—with cold, evil, yellow eyes. The most horrible one I'd seen yet.

It was screaming!

"Nooo!" I shrieked.

I hurled my cards at the window.

How did she do it?

How did Mrs. Marder work her evil magic on *my* cards? How did she see us with the shades pulled down?

We didn't stay at Max's long that afternoon. I was still shaking when we left his house.

"Are you okay?" Jeff asked me as we headed down Fear Street.

"No!" I shouted. "I'm not okay! I feel like a walking target. I got a joker. Now something terrible is going to happen to me. I'm just waiting for the rattles and hisses to start. I'm waiting for a bunch of jokers to attack me!"

"Take it easy, Brit," Jeff said. "We'll stay with you. They won't attack all of us."

"We'll walk you home," Louisa offered. "Don't worry."

They walked me all the way to my front door. "Thanks, guys," I told them. "You're really good friends."

For some reason, that sent Frankie into a fit of laughter.

"Frankie, quit it!" Louisa rolled her eyes. "You've been acting so weird lately. All you do is laugh. This isn't funny."

"Ha! Ha! The joke is on you," Frankie said, and started to laugh some more.

The laughter pounded in my head. "Cut it out, Frankie!" I yelled. I just couldn't stand the sound.

I broke away from the group and ran into my house. "Mom?" I called.

No answer.

78

"Mom?" I called again. My eyes searched the kitchen. There was no sign of my mom. And no sign that she'd been there.

No groceries. Nothing on the stove.

My heart began to race.

"MOM!" I screamed. "Where are you?"

No answer.

I turned and ran for the stairs.

"Jimmy?" I called. "Jimmy? Are you home?"

I waited to hear his voice.

But all I heard was a faint hissing sound.

Mom must be taking a shower, I tried to tell myself. *It's only the shower running.*

That's all.

Just the shower.

But the hissing sound grew louder—and turned into rattling.

I searched frantically for a place to hide.

All I could think of was the hall closet.

I dashed for it. I threw open the door—and screamed.

There they were—five ugly jokers in pointy green hats!

Waiting for me.

Leering at me with their hideous grins.

Each one held a stick—with a horrible, grinning skull perched on the top.

Their lips curled into an ugly sneer.

Then one moved forward. It raised its skull-stick high—then it lunged for me.

"Nooo!" I cried.

I dropped to the hall floor. I covered my head with my arms. I squeezed my eyes shut.

Three more jokers circled me. Danced around me. Swatted me with their skull-sticks.

They laughed and screamed. And chanted.

"All red and black must bow to green!
All red and black must bow to green!"

Over and over again.

I hugged my arms more tightly around my head.

They rattled their sticks wildly. Shrieking now. Shrieking madly.

Then all the noise stopped.

Gone. The jokers must be gone.

I slowly raised my head—and gasped.

They were still there! Hovering above me. Staring at me in eerie silence.

"Leave me alone!" I screamed. "Go away!"

The first joker stretched his hand toward me.

"Get away from me!" I cried, shrinking away.

But he yanked on my arm and pulled me to my feet.

I stared into his horrible eyes. And they began to glow an evil red.

"Wh-what are you going to do?" I stammered.

The joker glared at me. He lifted his skull-stick high in the air. The other jokers did the same.

They began to shake them again. More frantically than before.

The rattling was deafening.

I threw my hands over my ears. But I couldn't drown out the terrifying sound.

The skulls seemed to start breathing. A green mist poured from their nostrils. Their hollow cheeks began to pulse. And from deep within their sockets, their eyes began to glow.

The jokers started singing their horrible chant.

"We shake the skull with eyes that gleam!
　We make our marks, we laugh and scream!
　Her army strengthens day by day
　You play her game! She'll make you pay!
　All red and black must bow to green. . . ."

Then they stopped—and ran out of the house.

My legs collapsed underneath me.

I couldn't move.

I didn't even move when the front door began to open.

I only stared.

"Brittany!" my mom exclaimed as she and Jimmy walked through the door. "Why are you sitting on the floor?"

I didn't answer. What could I say?

Mom held out a hand to help me.

"Where were you, Mom?" I asked quietly. "I came home and nobody was here."

"Jimmy had a late doctor's appointment," she replied. "It was the only one we could get. I told you about it this morning."

"You did? I—I guess I wasn't listening."

I knew I wasn't listening. For the last week all I'd been thinking about was Mrs. Marder and her hideous jokers.

"Hey, Brit?" Jimmy said. "Want to see my new card trick?"

"Not now!" I yelled. A deck of cards was the last thing I wanted to see—

But then I changed my mind.

I was beginning to get an idea—

"Sure, Jimmy," I said. "I'll watch your new trick later."

I turned toward the stairs. "Mom, I'm not hungry. I think I'll go up to my room."

I gripped the banister and slowly began to climb the steps.

"Hey, Brit?" Jimmy called after me. "What's that thing on your arm?"

I glanced down.

My pulse suddenly thundered in my ears.

There it was.

Dark and clear.

The sign of the club.

18

The next morning before school, I found Jeff by his locker.

"Take a look." I held out my arm and pushed up my sleeve.

"Oh!" he moaned. "The jokers got you! But how?"

I told him all about it. Including the new line of the rhyme.

"I'm really scared," I admitted, shuddering.

"So am I," Jeff said. "And Frankie is acting totally crazy."

"I know," I agreed. "The jokers have gotten him three times now. That's enough to make anyone crazy, I guess."

"You know, I was thinking—he seems to get worse with each mark on his arm," Jeff pointed out.

I stared at him. "You're right. I didn't realize it—but you're right!"

"Maybe we should talk to Mr. Emerson," Jeff suggested. "We'll tell him we can't go to Max's anymore."

"It'll never work," I said gloomily. "We can't tell him what's happening. He'll think we're all crazy. Or worse—he'll say that we made up the story to get out of going. Then we'll really be in trouble."

"Yeah, that's true. Okay. We'll go to Max's this afternoon," Jeff told me. "But we have to say *no more cards*. And we have to mean it!"

"Right," I declared. "No cards, no jokers."

Usually the school day seemed to drag by so slowly. But the one day I wanted to last forever whizzed by. I couldn't believe it when the three-thirty bell rang.

"So who's going to break the news to Mrs. Davidson and Max?" I asked as we headed toward Fear Street. "Who's going to tell them we're not playing cards?"

"I'll do it," Jeff volunteered. "And I won't let them talk us into changing our minds."

We turned a corner. Mrs. Marder's house loomed in the distance. No way were we going to cut through her yard today!

We hurried past her gate—and the cats hissed at us.

"They're really hissing loudly!" Louisa quickened her step.

Louisa was right. I'd never heard her cats hiss this loud before. And it seemed to be getting louder.

"Wait!" Louisa cried. "It's not the cats! Look!"

Louisa pointed a trembling finger at some bushes ahead.

Jokers!

Six horrible jokers jumped out from behind the shrubs.

We froze in place.

The jokers leapt forward.

Circled us.

They rattled their skulls in our faces.

And began their awful chant:

"We shake the skull with eyes that gleam!
  We make our marks, we laugh and scream!
  Her army strengthens day by day,
  You play her game! She'll make you pay!
  All red and black must bow to green. . . .
  For she alone is now our queen!"

"Let's get out of here!" Jeff yelled.

We broke through the horrible circle—and ran.

The jokers came after us. One of them whacked Louisa with its skull-stick.

"Split up!" I screamed.

We broke off in different directions.

I darted across the street. So did Frankie. Then we ran opposite ways. I glanced over my shoulder.

None of the jokers were chasing me.

Oh, no! They were *all* after Frankie.

What were they going to do to him?

19

I spun and ran after him. "We have to help Frankie!" I cried to the others.

The jokers grabbed Frankie. They held him by his arms and legs—and dragged him down the street.

They pulled him into the vacant lot across from Mrs. Marder's. The lot with the big hole in the ground.

Jeff and Louisa raced over to me. Louisa was clutching her arm.

"Brit! It got me!" she cried. "One of the jokers hit my arm and—look!"

Next to the club on Louisa's arm was a diamond.

"Help!" Frankie's cry rang out from the lot. "Help me!"

We raced over to the lot. But when we got there, Frankie was nowhere to be seen. Neither were the jokers.

"Frankie?" my voice shook. "Where are you?"

As if answering me, the jokers popped out of the hole.

They laughed an evil laugh. They shook their skull-sticks hard. Then they ran off.

Louisa, Jeff, and I ran to the edge of the hole. We peered in. Frankie stood at the bottom, staring down.

"Frankie?" Jeff called. "You can come up. They're gone."

Frankie didn't move.

"Come on, Frankie. It's really okay," I said.

Frankie stared down, motionless.

"You're scaring me, Frankie!" Louisa cried.

"Let's pull him out," Jeff suggested.

The three of us leaned over the hole. We grabbed Frankie's arms.

"One, two, three!" Jeff called, and we pulled.

Frankie didn't fight us. But he didn't help either. We struggled—but we finally tugged him out.

Jeff, Louisa, and I fell back on the ground, trying to catch our breath.

Frankie sat in the dirt, staring into space.

"Oh, no!" Louisa cried. "Look! Frankie's arm!"

I was afraid to look. But I did.

89

There it was.

A heart.

"Oh, no, Frankie," I moaned. "You have all four suits!"

What will happen now? I wondered. What will those horrible jokers do to him next?

Frankie glanced up, as if reading my thoughts.

I gazed into his face—and screamed.

His eyes bulged from their sockets.

His mouth twisted in a horrible grin.

His tongue hung out of his mouth.

"Frankie!" I cried. I turned frantically to Jeff and Louisa.

They were staring at Frankie in horror. They began to shrink away from him.

I turned back.

"Frankie?" I gasped.

He seemed to have shrunk.

He wore a shiny black clown suit. And a green floppy hat with bells at the tip. And little green pointy shoes.

Frankie grinned horribly at us.

Only he wasn't Frankie anymore.

20

He was a joker!

Frankie opened his mouth and let out a terrible scream.

Then he whirled around and ran off, laughing.

He headed for Fear Street.

"Let's follow him!" I yelled.

We chased him as he ran down the street, letting out little shrieks.

He ran fast. Faster than we could.

He ran to the end of the street and turned.

When we reached the corner, he was gone.

"That was so awful!" Louisa moaned. "Poor Frankie!"

"That's what will happen to *us* if we don't stop Mrs. Marder!" I exclaimed.

"We should go to Max's house right now," Louisa declared. "And call the police."

We turned down Fear Street and ran on to Max's.

It felt strange to be standing on his porch without Frankie.

Louisa rang the bell.

No one answered.

Louisa pressed the bell again—but no one came to the door.

"That's weird," Jeff said. "Mrs. Davidson knew we were coming."

I pounded on the door. As I did, it opened. I stuck my head in. "Mrs. Davidson?" I called.

She didn't answer.

"We have to hurry!" Louisa exclaimed. "Mrs. Davidson won't mind if we go in and call the police."

"Right," Jeff agreed. "This is an emergency!"

We hurried inside.

"First let's see if Max is in his room," I suggested. "He might get frightened if he hears someone in the house."

We ran down the hall to Max's room.

Max sat in his bed, wearing his white pajamas. Shuffling a deck of cards.

"Max?" I spoke softly so I wouldn't startle him. "Hi!"

He turned to face us. "Oh, hi," he greeted us. "Want to play Hearts?"

"No!" Louisa exclaimed. She rushed over to his bed. "You know those awful jokers, Max?"

He nodded.

"They came alive. They attacked Frankie," Louisa told him. "And he changed! Right in front of us, Frankie turned into a joker!"

Max's pale blue eyes grew wide with fright. I hoped hearing bad news wasn't going to make him sicker.

"We have to use your phone," Jeff put in. "We have to call the police."

"The phone's in the kitchen, right?" I asked him.

But Max didn't answer. He was mumbling something. At first I couldn't understand him. But slowly the words became clear.

"She's done it!" Max was saying. "She's done it! She's done it!" He chanted over and over.

"Max!" I cried. "Stop that! You're making it worse!"

Max's eyes turned to meet mine.

"Don't you see, Brittany?" he asked softly. "She's done it! It's too late. We're all doomed. All of us!"

21

"**M**ax!" I cried. "What are you saying? You're scaring me!"

But Max didn't answer me. He kept repeating, "We're doomed. We're doomed." I wondered if he had a fever or something.

Luckily, at that moment, Mrs. Davidson appeared in the doorway of his room.

"Hi, kids!" she exclaimed. "Sorry I wasn't here when you arrived. But I'm glad you came today!" She smiled as she walked into the room.

"Mrs. Davidson, we have to call the police," Louisa blurted out. "Something awful has happened to Frankie!"

"They got him!" Jeff sputtered. "They got Frankie!"

"Who got him?" Mrs. Davidson cried.

"They got him!" Jeff repeated. He was getting more upset by the second. "They got him!"

Mrs. Davidson gasped. "Has he been kidnapped?"

We all started talking at once then.

"Wait! Wait!" she cried. "If Frankie's been kidnapped, I'd better call the police right now!"

"Yes!" we all cried. "Call the police!"

Mrs. Davidson hurried from the room.

I let out a huge sigh of relief.

At last someone was helping us!

"She's done it," Max kept muttering. "She's done it!"

"Take it easy, Max," I said. "Everything is going to be okay now."

Max gazed up at me with his pale blue eyes. "She's crazy, Brittany," he whispered. "Completely crazy. You know that, don't you?"

"I know she's evil," I said. "Poor Frankie! Maybe that's where he ran. Maybe he ran to her house—"

"Brittany?" Louisa cut in. "Mrs. Davidson doesn't really know what happened. I think *we* should talk to the police. We have to tell them everything—right now! The sooner we tell them, the sooner they can help Frankie!"

"That makes sense," I said. "I'll catch Mrs. Davidson before she hangs up."

I ran down the hall. As I neared the kitchen, I heard Mrs. Davidson's voice through the door.

"No, Officer," she was saying. "These kids wouldn't lie! They wouldn't say their friend had been kidnapped if he hadn't been!"

Mrs. Davidson sure was sticking up for us!

I pushed open the kitchen door. Mrs. Davidson had her back to me.

"Why, Officer!" she exclaimed. "That's a terrible thing to say. I assure you these kids are not making this up!"

I opened my mouth to say something to Mrs. Davidson.

Then I closed it.

I stared at Mrs. Davidson.

I tried to make sense of what I saw.

But I couldn't.

"Yes, Officer," Mrs. Davidson said. "You have my word."

Mrs. Davidson was talking.

But she wasn't on the phone.

The phone hung on the wall across the room from Mrs. Davidson.

It was an old phone.

Too old to be a speakerphone.

"Can you come and talk to these kids, Officer?" Mrs. Davidson asked. "Yes, right this minute. The sooner you get here, the sooner you can get to work on this case."

But Mrs. Davidson wasn't talking to the police. She wasn't talking to anyone!

22

I stood there, frozen.

I stared at Mrs. Davidson's back as she pretended to talk to the police.

I stared at her beautiful apple-green blouse and her dark green slacks . . . and her green suede shoes. . . .

And gasped.

You play her game! She'll make you pay!
All red and black must bow to green. . . .
For she alone is now our queen!

I backed silently out of the kitchen. I let the door close without a sound.

Then I turned and charged up to Max's room. I shut the door behind me.

"Brittany!" Louisa cried. "What's wrong? You look pale."

"I—I went into the kitchen," I croaked. "Mrs. Davidson didn't see me. She was talking—telling the police to come. But, Louisa—she wasn't on the phone! She was only pretending to make the call!"

Now it was Louisa's and Jeff's turn to look scared.

"Max?" I said. "Does this make sense to you?"

"That's what I've been trying to tell you," Max cried. "She's crazy!"

"You mean you were talking about your mom?" I demanded.

"She's not my mom," Max whispered.

23

"**W**hat?" Jeff, Louisa, and I all cried.

"I'm not sick either," Max went on. "I never had pneumonia. I'm her prisoner. She uses me to get players for her card games. She's some kind of evil sorceress."

"Does she have magical powers?" Louisa asked. Her voice trembled.

Max nodded. "Her magic depends on the jokers. The more jokers she has, the stronger her powers are."

"I can't believe this!" I cried. "Mrs. Davidson is so—so nice! She's always smiling!" I put my hand to my head, trying to piece things together. "And Mrs. Marder! You're telling us Mrs.

Marder *isn't* behind any of this. It's Mrs. Davidson!"

Max nodded sadly.

Then I had a horrible thought. I gazed from Louisa to Jeff to Max. "Oh, no! Frankie! He must be part of her army of jokers now!"

"Yes, he is," Max said. "It's horrible. She tricks kids like you into playing cards. Then she makes sure one of you draws a joker. Once you draw a joker, the attacks begin. For every attack, the jokers mark you with a card suit. When you have all four suits, you turn into a joker too."

I started shaking badly. I sat down on Max's bed.

"Are the jokers all under her power?" I asked.

Max nodded. "They're completely helpless. They have to do whatever she says."

"How many kids has she trapped this way?" Jeff asked.

"Frankie makes thirteen," Max said. "Shadyside is the fourth town we've moved to. She'll try to get all of you into her army. Then we'll move again. To another town nearby. And Mrs. Davidson—except that she'll think up a new name—will go to another school. She'll talk to the principal. She'll ask if kids can come and visit her poor, sick son."

"But, Max," Jeff said, frowning, "there's one thing I don't get."

"What's that?" Max asked.

"How do *you* fit into this?"

For a moment, Max didn't say anything.

Then he held out his left arm. He shoved up his pajama sleeve. There, above his wrist, were three marks: a club, a diamond, and a spade.

"See—I'm only one sign away from becoming a joker," he said. "If I don't help her, she'll turn me into one. I'm sorry I didn't help you. I didn't know what to do."

"We can still escape, can't we?" I asked him. "We're not jokers yet. If we get out of here—right now—we can call the police for real."

"Brittany's right," Louisa whispered. "Let's go—quick! Before she comes back!"

"Come on, Max," Jeff said. "You're coming with us."

Max threw back his covers and climbed out of bed. The four of us ran for the door.

But we didn't make it.

There in the doorway stood Mrs. Davidson.

As always, she was smiling. But now it was a crooked, wicked smile. In her hand she held a scepter with a hideous skull at the top.

"Going somewhere?" she asked.

She stepped into Max's room.

We backed up.

"I don't think so," she answered herself.

"We—we have to get home," Louisa whimpered.

"Sit down!" she snarled. "Nobody is going anywhere. It's time to play my game!"

24

Mrs. Davidson shoved us toward the table.

My heart pounded like crazy.

I could hardly breathe.

We sat down at the table. Mrs. Davidson sat next to me—in the place where Frankie used to sit.

Max was right—we were doomed.

"You're too nosy, Brittany," Mrs. Davidson told me as she picked up the cards. "How dare you spy on me in my kitchen?"

My stomach tightened into a knot.

Mrs. Davidson shuffled the cards at lightning speed.

"Because of you, I have to hurry up my plans. How I'll enjoy turning you into the most hideous joker in the whole deck!"

She cackled loudly. "Before I deal the cards, I have a surprise for you."

The knot in my stomach grew tighter. What now?

Her evil green eyes flicked from Jeff to Louisa to me.

"Today I've put *ten* jokers in the deck! Yes! This will speed things up, kids! Let me see. Brittany— you need three jokers. Two for you, Louisa. And four for Jeff. And Max? All you need is one more!"

Mrs. Davidson threw back her head and shrieked with laughter. "By the end of the game," she went on, "I'll have four new jokers in my army! Hey, kids! Want to see what you'll look like? Here, take a peek!"

Mrs. Davidson began pulling joker cards from the top of the deck. Jokers I hadn't seen before.

One had rotted fangs.

One had green drool oozing from its lips.

But the worst one was a joker I *had* seen before. It was the one Max had dealt me the last time we played. The one with the yellow eyes.

Mrs. Davidson tapped that awful joker with a long fingernail. "Take a good look at this one, Brittany," she snarled. "I had this face in mind for your new look!"

Mrs. Davidson plucked two cards out of the deck and pushed them to the middle of the table.

"Now there are fifty cards left in the deck," she told us. "We'll each get ten."

She began shuffling again. "Ten jokers! My, this will be an exciting game, don't you think? You know, I have a way with cards. A way to make sure you each get the perfect hand—just the right amount of jokers!"

She shuffled the cards some more. "Yes—I'll make sure I deal the cards right—especially for you, my little Max!" She glared across the table at him. "My little traitor!"

Her expression grew fierce. "You think I don't know what you told your friends? I know everything, Max dear! Everything!"

"There," she said, placing the deck in front of me. "Cut the cards, Brittany."

I reached for the cards. My hand shook so badly, I dropped half the deck on the floor.

"You stupid, clumsy girl!" Mrs. Davidson screeched.

Then she drew back her skull-scepter and swung it at me!

25

"**N**oooo!" I screamed as I dropped to the floor.

The skull-scepter grazed the top of my head.

I darted under the table. "Leave me alone!" I screamed.

"Get out from there. And pick up those cards!" Mrs. Davidson ordered. "NOW!"

I tried to pick them up. But they kept dropping out of my trembling hands.

"Hurry!" Mrs. Davidson kicked at me with her green shoe. "We haven't got all day! After I get my four new jokers, we have to pack. We're moving again, Max dear!"

Finally I crawled out from under the table.

I placed the deck in front of Mrs. Davidson. Then I cut the cards.

My heart pounded as I watched Mrs. Davidson start to deal.

I flinched with each card she slapped down in front of me.

Each card might be the awful joker! The joker that had my new, horrible face.

"Now, pick up your hands, kids!" Mrs. Davidson commanded.

My pulse thumped like a drum as I pushed my cards together. I gathered them into a stack. But I didn't pick them up.

I glanced around the table.

My friends stared down at their cards in fear. No one picked up a hand.

Mrs. Davidson's green eyes darted eagerly from player to player. Our fright brought a cheery smile to her face.

"Look at your cards!" Mrs. Davidson shouted.

Slowly, I picked up my hand.

Slowly, I turned it around—and let out a sigh.

The two of hearts.

Nine more cards to go.

With a shaky finger I pushed the two of hearts aside.

Six of clubs!

I glanced around at the other players. Jeff had half his fan open. He seemed okay. So he must not have found a joker yet.

Louisa was still staring at the first card in her hand. Across the table Max held his cards face-down in his pale, trembling hands. One joker—and he was doomed!

Mrs. Davidson hadn't even straightened her pile. No, she was far too interested in how we'd scream and cry when we discovered our jokers.

I took a deep breath.

I held my thumb against the six of clubs.

My heart raced. I forced myself to push aside the six.

I saw a face!

I opened my mouth to scream!

I stared down at my hand.

The face belonged to a jack. The jack of diamonds.

"Ohhh," I moaned with relief.

"Did you get a joker?" shrieked Mrs. Davidson. "Did you?"

"No," I croaked.

"Me either," Louisa whispered.

Jeff shook his head no.

Max only shrugged. He didn't have the nerve to look at his cards.

I glanced back at my hand.

Three cards down.

Seven to go.

I didn't know if I could stand it!

Quickly, I exposed my fourth card.

Eight of spades.

Whew!

"This is no fun!" Mrs. Davidson screamed. "You're wasting time! Open your hands quickly! That's good card manners! Do it! Look at *all* your cards right now!"

"You're not looking at *your* cards!" I shouted at her. *"You* don't have good card manners!"

"All right, Brittany!" Mrs. Davidson spat out my name.

She grabbed her cards with both hands. She shoved them together and picked them up.

"This is good card manners," she said. "This is the way you open your hand—quickly, like this."

She rapidly fanned her cards.

"What?" she shrieked. "No! This is impossible!"

"What?" Louisa cried.

Mrs. Davidson's eyes grew wild. The veins in her neck bulged out. She screamed, "Noooooo!"

I shrank back in my chair.

Mrs. Davidson's face turned red with fury. She glared at me with her crazed eyes. Then she stood up from the table—and threw her whole hand up in the air.

I watched with a dry mouth as her ten cards floated down.

A bead of sweat trickled down my cheek as they fluttered to the table.

I forced myself to look at them as they landed.

I gasped.

On the table lay ten hideous jokers.

26

No one moved. We all stared at the jokers.

The room turned silent—until the hissing started. Faint at first. Then growing louder—quickly.

And louder still—as a band of jokers burst through the door—screaming.

We jumped up from our chairs and huddled in a corner of the room. But that wasn't really necessary.

The jokers were after only one card player.

Mrs. Davidson.

They circled around her, shaking their skulls.

"Get away!" Mrs. Davidson cried. "Obey me at once!"

But the jokers only laughed and screamed more loudly.

"Obey your queen!" she cried. "Stand back!"

A joker with a toothy grin swatted at her with the skull on his stick.

As the jokers danced around her, I tried to study each one's face.

Which one was Frankie? I thought he might be the one with the twisted grin—the joker card he'd drawn. But there was nothing of Frankie in that awful face.

"Look, Brit," Louisa whispered. "They're picking her up!"

"Put me down, you idiots!" Mrs. Davidson cried as the jokers lifted her up over their heads. "I made you what you are!" she shrieked. "You are nothing without me. Nothing!"

Her words didn't frighten the jokers at all. They shook their skulls and hooted with laughter as they carried their queen from the room.

And they were gone.

For a moment no one spoke.

Then all four of us cried out with relief.

We were safe! We weren't going to turn into jokers!

"What amazing luck!" Jeff exclaimed as we let go

of each other. "I can't believe Mrs. Davidson got all ten jokers."

"Well, *luck* had a little help," I told him.

"What do you mean?" Jeff asked.

"When I dropped the cards, I stacked the deck," I explained.

Louisa looked confused. "You did what?"

"Stacked the deck," I repeated. "That's when you put the cards in a special order. It's an old card trick. I asked Jimmy to show me how to do it last night. But I was pretty scared. I wasn't sure I got it right."

"Wow," Jeff said. "Nice work, Brittany."

"Excellent!" Louisa agreed, slapping me a high-five.

"If it weren't for you," Max added, "I'd be a joker now."

"Let's get out of here," I said, shivering. "I don't know what's happening with Mrs. Davidson and the jokers. But I don't think we should stick around to find out."

We ran out of Max's room and down the stairs to the front door.

I reached out for the doorknob.

I twisted it. It turned easily in my hand.

But before I could pull the door open, a horrible hissing filled the room.

I turned.

The jokers! They were back!

They lunged at us. Circled us, cutting us off from the door.

They grinned their evil grins.

They rattled their hideous skull-sticks.

Then they closed in around us. The joker with the toothy grin stepped toward me.

"The—the game's over!" I stammered.

But the joker didn't care.

He kept coming toward me, rattling his skull-stick.

"Run!" Max cried.

We charged through the circle and ran back to Max's room.

We slammed the door behind us.

"We made it!" Louisa exclaimed. "We got past the jokers!"

Jeff frowned. "It was too easy. They let us run back here."

Jeff had a point.

Of course the jokers wanted us in this room. It had no outside door. There was no way out. We were trapped!

"What do we do now?" I croaked.

"We wait," Max said.

"Wait?" I cried. "For what? For the jokers to show up?"

115

"Exactly." Max calmly held a stack of cards in his hand. He ran his thumb over the edges.

"Ohhh!" I groaned.

Why had I trusted Max?

He played cards for Mrs. Davidson.

He helped her trap kids. Trap *us!*

And we had just let him trap us again!

27

Outside Max's room I heard the hissing start.

Max glanced toward the door. I lunged for him. I tried to grab the cards out of his hand.

"Stop, Brittany!" Max cried. He twisted away from me. "You don't know what you're doing!"

I could hardly hear him over the horrible rattling skulls.

The jokers stormed into the room. I clapped my hands over my ears. Their crazed laughter was like thunder.

They laughed and laughed. And why not? They had us right where they wanted us.

"You!" Max called. He was talking to a joker. The joker with the toothy grin.

Max held the joker's card up.

As the joker glanced at himself on the card, Max turned the card sideways and ripped it in half.

Instantly the joker's skull-stick turned into mist—then vanished into thin air.

His face began to droop. Melt.

I turned to Max. "Wh-what's going on?" I stammered.

Max didn't answer. His eyes remained glued to the joker.

I turned back—and gasped.

The joker's face wasn't melting. It was—changing. Changing into the face of a boy.

His nose, his cheeks, his chin, all began to take on a new form. He was beginning to look like a regular boy.

I watched in awe as his horrible red eyes turned a normal shade of blue. As his teeth shrank to a regular size.

Suddenly the rattling of skulls filled the room.

The other jokers!

I had forgotten about them!

They shrieked loudly—and charged at us.

"Max—quick! The other jokers!" I shouted.

Max shoved some joker cards in my hand. Louisa and Jeff grabbed some too.

"Make sure they're looking at the card when you rip it!" Max cried.

We ripped our cards—and all the jokers turned back into kids. All but one.

I held the last joker card in my hand.

Frankie's joker card.

I held it up.

The joker that was Frankie darted around the room—shrieking madly.

"Hey, Frankie," I shouted. "Look!"

The joker turned my way.

I held up the card—and ripped it in half.

The joker's face began to change.

In moments Frankie was back.

All the kids who had been jokers thanked us for helping them. They called their parents, and we waited for them to arrive to take them home.

Finally a couple with blond hair and pale blue eyes hurried up Mrs. Davidson's walk. Max zoomed out of the house. I think the three of them broke the record for the world's longest hug.

"Thanks, Brittany," Max said before he left. "You sure know how to stack a deck."

"Thank *you*, Max," I told him. "You sure know how to play your cards right!"

28

The next night Frankie called me. I stretched across my bed talking to him.

"You know what, Brit?" Frankie asked. "Jeff and I went over to Mrs. Marder's after school today. Jeff had to deliver some groceries." He coughed, sounding embarrassed. "I thought maybe I should apologize to her. You know. For the birdbath and stuff."

"You're kidding!" I exclaimed.

"Nope. Anyhow," Frankie hurried on, "Jeff asked her about her telescope. Know what? Before they retired, she and her husband both worked as astronomers! There's a cluster of stars somewhere about a billion miles away that's named after them. It's called the Marder Formation!"

"Really?" I said. "But wait a second. Why was her telescope aimed at Max's window?"

"You saw how her cats jumped up on everything," Frankie reminded me. "They must have knocked it out of line. And did you know she *rescued* all those cats?" he went on. "None of them had homes. They would have been put to sleep if she hadn't adopted them. She goes out at night sometimes, looking for strays."

That must have been what she was doing in the woods outside Louisa's house! I groaned. "Now I feel terrible for believing those awful stories about her," I said.

There was a loud knock at my door.

"It's me!" Jimmy called. "I've got a great card trick to show you, Brit!"

"Did you hear that?" I asked Frankie. "Well, Jimmy did show me how to stack a deck. So I guess I owe it to him to let him show me his latest card trick."

Frankie laughed. "Have fun, Brit!"

We hung up. "Come in!" I called to Jimmy. I patted the place next to me on my bed. I was in a great mood that night. If Jimmy had ten new card tricks, I promised myself, I'd watch them all.

"Okay," Jimmy said, plopping down on my bed. "Pick a card! Any card!"

He fanned a deck for me.

121

I slid a card out of the middle. "Should I look at it?" I asked him.

"Definitely," Jimmy said.

I turned the card over.

I stared at it. My mouth suddenly went dry.

I didn't want to believe what I was seeing.

It was a joker!

The most awful joker I'd ever seen!

It had bulging green eyes.

And a piggish, turned-up nose.

And wild, wiry hair.

Its big, evil smile spread from ear to ear. A smile formed by red, lipsticked lips.

It was Mrs. Davidson!

A golden crown rested on her hideous head.

Mrs. Davidson—the Queen of the Jokers.

I watched in horror as the queen opened her wide red mouth and let out a horrible scream.

My mouth opened too.

And I screamed and screamed.

GHOSTS OF FEAR STREET®

FIELD OF SCREAMS

FIELD OF SCREAMS

I stood with the bat over my shoulder and the ball in my left hand. I narrowed my eyes and glared down the field at my friend Eve.

"Are you ready for a hot one?" I yelled.

"You couldn't hit a hot one with a big old frying pan, Sanders!" Eve teased me. "You're such a weenie!"

"Weenie, huh?" I retorted. I ran my hand through my curly brown hair. I dug my foot into the dirt to get a good stance. Shifting my balance, I lofted the ball and hit a screaming grounder straight at Eve.

She went down with her glove and tried to stop it. But the ball took a wicked hop and skipped right through her mitt.

"Who's the weenie now, butterfingers?" I yelled.

The ball stopped about ten feet behind Eve. Her dark braids bounced as she jogged over and snatched it up. "You hit it weird, Buddy," she complained, throwing it back. "The next one won't get by me!"

I plucked the baseball easily from the air. "Those balls get by you so much, I think your glove is made of Swiss cheese!"

"Lay off, okay?" Eve grumbled.

Sometimes, I guess, I tease her a little too much.

"You took your eyes off the ball," I reminded her. "Remember what Coach Burress says. Follow the ball into your glove."

I hit another to her, not quite so hard this time.

Eve missed it. Again.

I shook my head. I'd been trying to help Eve with her fielding for three weeks, but it was no use. I had to face the facts. Eve was an awesome friend. But she was a lousy ballplayer.

The trouble was, *everybody* on the Shadyside Middle School baseball team was lousy. Everybody but me. And I was sick of it.

Just once, I thought as Eve ran over to the ball. Just once I'd like to play on a really good team. Is that too much to ask?

But no. This was our team's third season—and it smelled like another loser.

I felt bad about being annoyed at Eve. It wasn't her fault she couldn't play. She always tried her best. She was great at soccer and basketball. But baseball just wasn't in her.

"Sorry, Buddy," she called. "I'll get it next time."

"Sure. I'll hit you some flies for a while." Eve was pretty good at catching those.

And at least I was doing my favorite thing in the world—playing ball. School was out for the summer, and for once my mom didn't have any chores for me to do. Like mowing the grass or cleaning out the garage.

Eve and I were playing in an empty field that backed onto some of the older houses on Fear Street. These tall gray houses towered up above high wooden fences. They looked menacing and spooky. There was one in particular that got to me. It had dark windows like eyes that watched us play.

I was careful hitting the ball. I didn't want to have to go find it in one of those yards.

Not that Fear Street scared me. Sure, I'd heard all those stories about it—about ghosts in the cemetery and weird things in Fear Lake. But I didn't believe them.

Well, not really.

The more I hit the ball to Eve, the more that gloomy old house bothered me. Was someone really watching me behind those windows? It felt like it.

I tossed the ball up again and gave another swing. My aluminum bat connected with a *clang*.

3

The ball leapt off the bat like a rocket. I stared at it in surprise. I didn't realize I had taken such a big swing.

The ball shot through the air as if Cecil Fielder hit it. Eve craned her neck to watch it sail over her head.

"Oh, no!" I yelled. The ball disappeared over the fence.

Right into the one place I hoped it wouldn't go.

The backyard of that spooky house on Fear Street.

2

I stared at the creepy old house for a second.

Then I sprinted over to Eve. I'm short, but I move fast. I reached her in a few seconds.

"Wow!" she said as I ran up. "You really nailed that ball. No way could I have hit one that far!"

I just shrugged. I don't usually hit them that far either. But I wasn't about to admit that.

We jogged toward the fence. Its cedar boards stood warped with age. There were lots of holes to look through. I cupped my hands around my eyes to peek into the yard.

"Do you see the ball?" Eve asked.

"Nope," I answered. "Just a bunch of old junk."

I stepped back and studied the fence. I found a

5

place where the boards were loose. I shoved them aside.

"What are you doing?" Eve asked nervously.

"I'm going in to find my ball," I told her.

"Forget it, Buddy," Eve urged. "This place is creepy."

I rolled my eyes. "You don't believe all that Fear Street stuff, do you?"

Eve's cheeks turned red. "Don't you?"

"Hah! No way!" I said as I squeezed through the gap in the fence.

Well, I didn't. Not really.

"What a mess," I muttered as I looked the place over. Old pieces of machinery and broken furniture lay everywhere. No grass or trees grew. Just dirt and a few weeds here and there.

I glanced up at the house. Eve was right. It was pretty gruesome. Just the kind of place you'd expect a ghost or monster to live in. That is, if you believed in ghosts or monsters.

"Hurry up, Buddy," Eve whispered through the fence.

I moved toward the back porch. It was built up off the ground about three feet. I bent to peek underneath. Nothing but piled-up leaves and dirt. But then I caught a glimpse of white. Way back under the porch. My ball!

I got on my hands and knees and crawled after it. The day was so bright that when I ducked under the porch into the darkness I couldn't see a thing. I blinked a few times, and my eyes adjusted.

"Gross," I said as I moved forward. A horrible stink invaded my nose. It smelled like a sewer. I saw a big pipe way in the back with a crack in it. Thick brown goo seeped out.

I pinched my nose shut. The sooner you get the ball, the sooner you can get out of here, I thought. I started toward it again. Something sticky brushed against my forehead.

I reached up and pulled at whatever it was.

Ugh! A clump of cobweb came off in my hand. I reached up again to feel my hair. Webs stuck to it in thick gobs.

Something tickled the back of my neck. I swiped at it. A spider fell from my neck to the ground. "Oh, man," I moaned.

Then I felt more tickling. Like things moving in my hair, crawling across my ears. I swatted at them.

Dozens of little spiders swarmed over my fingers!

I fell flat on the ground, slapping at my head with both hands. "Get off me!" I yelled. "Get off me!"

When I was pretty sure I'd gotten rid of them all, I breathed a sigh of relief.

What am I, nuts? I thought. Who cares about the baseball? I have another one at home. This place is bad news. I'm leaving.

But then I glanced ahead of me. The ball was within reach. All I had to do was grab it.

I stretched out as far as I could. My fingertips touched the ball. I rolled it toward me. I almost had it. . . .

Something cold and hard suddenly locked around my ankle. "Yipe!" I squawked, and tried to jerk away.

Whatever had me held on tight. I felt it pulling at me. I kicked with my free foot. But the grip was like iron!

It dragged me backward. I fought as hard as I could. But it was no use. I was helpless.

I was caught!

3

I slid backward so fast, my face scraped against the dirt. I tried to yell, but dry leaves filled my mouth.

Then bright sunlight hit my face, blinding me. I blinked hard, trying to make my eyes adjust, but they wouldn't. Whatever had me in its clutches, I couldn't see it. The thing grabbed my shoulder. I felt myself being lifted up off the ground.

Finally, my eyes began to focus. I lifted my head and stared into the face of a wrinkled old man. He gazed down at me with cold, dark eyes. Only a few wisps of gray hair dotted his bald head. His lips parted, and I could see stained, yellowed teeth.

He was holding me three feet above the ground. His hands clamped my shoulders like vises. I squirmed, trying to get loose, but he hung on. Talk about strong!

"What are you doing under my house? You looking for something?" he demanded in a hoarse, rough voice.

"Let me down. Ow! Let me down!" I yelled. My heart pounded in my ears. What did this old man want with me?

Then, all of sudden, he let go. I fell to the ground and tumbled in the dirt.

"Ow!" I glared at him. "You didn't have to do that."

The man's lined face crinkled up like old paper as he grinned. He seemed to think I was funny.

"It's dangerous under that porch. I couldn't let you crawl under there. Besides, how do I know you're not trying to rob me? How do I know you aren't some kind of thief?"

"I am not a thief!" I protested. "I was just trying to get my baseball back. I got up and brushed the dirt from my pants and shirt. "I hit it over the fence by accident, and it rolled under your porch."

The old man's eyes narrowed. He scratched his chin.

"Baseball, huh?"

"It's the truth. I almost had it, when you grabbed me. If you don't believe me, look for yourself."

"I think I'll just do that," he said.

The old man grunted and crouched down on his hands and knees. He was wearing old, faded slacks and a suit jacket that dragged in the dirt as he peered under the porch.

He stuck his whole head underneath.

Maybe the spiders would get him, I thought. It would serve him right for scaring me.

He reached a hand back toward me, his head still under the porch. "Fetch me that rake by the wall."

I brought the old iron rake and put the handle in his hand. He stuck it under the porch and began to poke around.

"As I was saying, these old houses are dangerous, boy," he called up to me. He was under the porch up to his shoulders now. His bony rear stuck up in the air. "There's all kinds of stuff under here. Old rusty metal, black widow spiders . . ."

"Tell me about it," I muttered under my breath.

The old man started backing out. He drew out the rake. My baseball came with it. "There you go, son," he said, handing me the ball. "Next time, try fishing the ball out like I did, instead of diving under a stranger's porch without thinking."

I felt embarrassed now. Maybe he wasn't such a bad old guy after all.

"I guess you're right," I admitted. "Uh—thanks for getting my ball."

"What's your name, son?" the old man asked.

"Buddy Sanders," I answered.

"Ernie Ames. Call me Ernie," the old man said. He extended his hand to shake.

I grabbed it. It felt hard and scratchy, like sand-

11

paper. I pulled my hand away fast. I hoped he didn't notice.

I glanced back at the fence. Was Eve still watching?

"So you're a ballplayer, eh? You on a team?" he asked.

"Sure. I play third base for the Shadyside team."

Ernie grinned. "That's not a team. That's a joke."

"Aw, we do all right." I felt myself blush.

"Really? Won any games lately?"

I stared down at the dirt and dug around with my toe. "Well—not really."

"That's what I thought," he said.

I scowled. Okay, so it was a bonehead move for me to crawl under the guy's porch. But he didn't have to insult my team.

"So what?" I argued. "Just because the team isn't very good doesn't mean it isn't fun. And I can be a good third baseman even if my team doesn't always win."

Ernie's lips curled in a mean smile. "So you think you're pretty good, huh? Aren't you kind of short for a ballplayer?"

He was making me mad! I guess that's why I started bragging.

"Maybe I am short. But I'm good," I declared. "Coach thinks I'm the best third baseman he's ever had. Maybe the best ever to play for Shadyside."

"Impossible!" Ernie snorted. "Gibson was the best third baseman ever to play for Shadyside. Buddy

Gibson. He had it all—the glove, the bat . . ." He stared off into the distance as if he were remembering.

"Oh, yeah? Then how come I never heard of him?" I sneered.

The old man's gaze snapped back to mine. His eyes suddenly looked like two holes. Dark. Empty.

"Because for all his talent, Buddy Gibson was unlucky."

His voice sent chills through me. "Wh-what do you mean?"

Ernie leaned in close and whispered, "Buddy Gibson—and his whole team—were in the wrong place at the wrong time.

"And now they're buried in the Fear Street Cemetery!"

4

Buried in the Fear Street Cemetery?

I sucked in my breath. "You—you mean they all . . ."

Ernie Ames nodded.

"What happened to them?" I asked.

His face twisted as if he were in pain. "They were called the Doom Squad," he said slowly. "Folks called them that because they beat everybody. To play them meant doom. But once I—I mean once *they* had their accident, well—then they really *were* the Doom Squad. They all died. Every single one of them."

I shuddered. A whole baseball team—dead!

"What accident?" I asked. "How did it happen?"

Ernie turned without answering. He shuffled to the porch steps. "Wait here," he said.

"But—" I started to say.

Too late. He'd already gone inside. I ran over to the fence.

"Eve? Eve? Are you still there?" I called.

No one answered. Eve must have run off.

"Weenie," I muttered.

Should I take off myself? Ernie kind of gave me the creeps. On the other hand, I was curious about this Doom Squad.

Before I could make up my mind, Ernie came back out of the house. He shuffled down the porch steps, holding a shoe box. "Here we go," he said. "I've been saving these for years."

He pulled an old, creased paper from the box. I took it from him and stared at it. An old black-and-white picture of a kids' baseball team. Twelve guys—no girls. All about my age, twelve.

"That's the Doom Squad," Ernie explained. He moved behind me and pointed over my shoulder to different players.

"That one's Jimmy Grogan, the first baseman. Wade Newsom—he was the pitcher. Fielders Boog Johnson, Chad Weems, and Johnny Beans. Catcher, Billy Fein."

I checked the picture out. Everyone looked funny in their baggy, pin-striped uniforms. Their hats had little crowns with long bills. They look more like the *duck* squad than the Doom Squad, I thought.

"Which one is this Gibson kid?" I asked.

15

"That one." The old man's finger trembled as he pointed. "That's Gibson."

Buddy Gibson stared out of the photograph with a wide grin. He seemed more comfortable than the others, like he'd been born in that uniform.

Ernie must have guessed what I was thinking. "Looks like he belongs on a baseball card, doesn't he? Well, he did. Every player on that team was good, but Buddy was special. He had the real stuff. He was going to the majors."

I shifted uncomfortably. Did Ernie have to stand so close? His clothes had a funny, musty smell. Like they'd been sprinkled with soil or something.

"What year was this taken?" I asked.

"Nineteen forty-eight. Their last year. Right before the championship game."

"Did they win?" I asked.

"That's where the unluckiness comes in. They lost," the old man explained. "It was the bottom of the ninth. Bases were loaded and there were two outs. Shadyside led by two runs."

I nodded. I could picture it.

"A left-handed hitter came up to the plate. The coach moved everybody over, expecting him to hit the ball to the right, but he didn't. He hit a line drive to the left, down the third base line. It was a triple. Three runs scored. And Shadyside lost."

"Wow! That is a tough break," I agreed. "But why did it land them in the cemetery?"

"Losing the championship was only the beginning. There was supposed to be a party after the game for everyone—the winners and the losers. But the Doom Squad was so disappointed, they just left. On the way home their bus stalled on the railroad tracks. An oncoming train hit the bus. Killed them all."

"That's awful!" I gasped.

Ernie's lips were clamped tight. I didn't know what to say. He probably knew these guys.

Then he seemed to shake himself. "So tell me, what do you want, Buddy? What do you really want out of baseball?"

What a weird question. I shrugged. "Gee, I don't know. I want to be a pro ballplayer someday, I guess. Doesn't everybody?"

"No, I mean right now. What do you want most in the world?"

He stared at me. His burning gaze made me nervous. I guess that's why I suddenly blurted out the truth.

"I—I want to play on a *good* team for once. No—it's more than that. I want to play on the best Shadyside team ever!"

Ernie nodded slowly. Without another word he turned and walked back to his house. He opened the door to go inside.

He suddenly turned around. "I guessed that might be your wish," he said. "Who knows? Maybe it will come true."

A smile crossed his lips. He started to chuckle.

Then he ducked inside.

"What's so funny?" I called through the screen door.

Ernie didn't answer.

I waited there for a minute. But he never returned.

"Weird," I muttered to myself. I glanced around the mess of a yard. Might as well leave.

I peeked through the hole in the fence. Eve was long gone.

The shortest way home was down Fear Street, so I walked around to the front of Ernie's house. And bumped right into a policeman. The officer clapped a hand on my shoulder. "Are you all right?" he asked me.

"I'm fine," I answered, startled. "Is something wrong?"

Eve ran up behind him. "I called the police, Buddy."

"You what? Why'd you do that?" I demanded. Eve was sort of a scaredy-cat. But calling the cops? That was ridiculous.

"I saw that weird old man grab you when you were under the porch," Eve explained. "I thought you were in trouble."

Another voice called behind me, "I checked it out. There's no sign of anyone. The house is empty, just like it should be."

I turned and saw another policeman walking down

the front steps. He looked older than the first officer, maybe in his fifties.

"What do you mean?" I asked. "Some old guy lives there."

"I don't think so, son," the first officer told me. "This house is abandoned."

What? The place *was* shabby, but abandoned?

I turned and stared up at the old house.

Whoa!

Cream-colored paint hung down in long curls from warped old boards. The shutters dangled crookedly from rusty hinges. All the windows were boarded up. Ivy grew thickly over the whole thing.

"But—I don't get it. I just met the guy who lives here," I said.

"Not possible," the older police officer told me. "No one has lived here since 1948!"

5

Two days later we played the Oneiga Blue Devils. By the fourth inning we were behind five to one. It was another runaway. As usual, I had the only run on the team.

"I'm telling you, that old man was a ghost!" Eve insisted.

She sat beside me in the dugout, munching sunflower seeds. She thought it made her look like a pro. I hated to break it to her. But she looked about as much like a pro as my cat, Foster.

"Come on, Buddy," Eve continued. "Fear Street? An abandoned house? A disappearing old man? Hello? You figure it out."

"Would you get off it?" I snapped. "That was two days ago. And besides, we're playing a *game* here, remember? Maybe you should pay more attention to that."

"Whoa. What's your problem?" She spat out the shell of a sunflower seed.

I frowned. I shouldn't have yelled at her like that. "Sorry," I mumbled. "I just can't stand losing—again."

Inside, I knew that wasn't the only reason I yelled. Really, I didn't want to think about the whole Fear Street thing. I mean, what if Eve were right? What if that old guy *was* a ghost?

Not that I really believed in that stuff. But still . . .

It was a relief when I noticed that I was next at bat.

"Gotta go," I said. "I'm on deck." I trotted to the on-deck circle, grabbed a bat, and swung it around to loosen up.

My teammate Scott Adams stood at first. He made it there on an error. Glen Brody was up at the plate. Maybe we could actually get some runs this inning.

Seeing Scott and Glen reminded me again of Fear Street. Scott lived there. Glen went over to his house all the time. Nothing weird ever happened to them.

Or did it? I remembered Glen telling some wild story at school once. Something about a monster from Fear Lake—

I stopped thinking about it when Glen popped the ball up into short left field.

"Run!" I shouted.

The Oneiga shortstop ran back for the ball, but

he collided with the left fielder. Scott was already rounding second base. Heading for third. Glen made it to first and then chugged toward second.

Safe!

Two runners in scoring position. All right! I told myself. Time to show these suckers a little something.

I felt pumped up as I approached the plate. My teammates cheered me on from the dugout. "Do it, Buddy!" "Go for it, Buddy!"

I stepped into the batter's box, ready to send this sucker downtown. Over the fence. Never to be seen again.

I grinned at the pitcher and waggled my bat a few times over the plate. He wiped some sweat from his brow.

Getting nervous? I taunted the pitcher in my mind. You better be. I'm going to mail this ball to Mars!

The first pitch was way outside. I let it go and moved closer to the plate, crowding it.

"Try to give me an outside pitch now, chicken," I muttered.

The pitcher wound up again. I tightened my grip on the bat.

Then, from the corner of my eye, I glimpsed a familiar face.

Ernie Ames. The old man from the house on Fear Street.

He stood at the fence. Watching me.

His eyes burned into mine. I felt as if I couldn't tear my gaze away from him.

What did he want?

"Duck!" someone yelled.

My head whipped around. Oh, man!

The ball was speeding straight toward me!

Whack! The ball hit me and knocked me down. My head smacked into the ground.

Even though I was wearing a helmet, pain exploded in my head. I saw a huge flash of white light. Little stars danced in front of my eyes.

Then everything went black.

6

The next thing I heard was somebody calling my name.

"Buddy. Buddy, talk to me," someone called.

I opened my eyes slowly. Man, did my head hurt!

My vision was blurry for a second. As it cleared, I made out faces peering down at me. Strangers.

"You okay, Buddy? That pitch hit you square in the head."

The man speaking was tall. And he had dark hair he wore slicked back with some sort of shiny oil.

How does he know my name? I wondered. I've never seen him before.

"Oooh!" I groaned and sat up slowly. My head throbbed where the ball hit me. I felt a little dizzy.

"Thatta boy. Can you get up?"

24

Without waiting for an answer, the shiny-haired man grabbed my arms and hauled me to my feet. I stood, wobbling for a second.

"Feeling steadier? Good. Shake it off," the man told me.

Shake it off? I thought. Is he crazy? I just got clobbered in the head with a fastball!

"I—uh—" I started to say.

"Hit by the pitch—take your base!" the umpire yelled.

"But I—"

"Come on, tough guy!" the man with the slicked-back hair interrupted. "You heard the ump. Go take your base." He tucked his hand under my elbow and hustled me to first base. "Good, good," he muttered, and trotted away.

Who was that guy anyway?

I stood at first base and squeezed my eyes shut, trying to get over my feeling of confusion.

"Batter up!" the umpire called.

I opened my eyes to see who was next at bat.

Whoa. Hold up, I thought. Who is *that* guy? He doesn't play on my team! And what's with his uniform?

The pants were baggy. The shirt was loose. The whole outfit looked like a sack. And instead of the red, white, and blue colors of my Shadyside Middle School uniform, it was white with black pinstripes.

Come to think of it, my own uniform felt strangely heavy and loose. I glanced down.

Black and white pinstripes! I was wearing pin-stripes! How did that happen? Where was *my* uniform?

Before I could think, the batter hit a grounder toward the shortstop. I took off from first base. The ball skipped past the shortstop and into the outfield.

I rounded second at full speed, really running now. I slid into the bag and barely beat the throw to third.

I stood and brushed myself off. A rough hand clapped me on the shoulder.

"Way to hustle, Gibson," a deep voice said in my ear.

Gibson? Who was Gibson? I turned—and found myself staring at a man with a heavy red face.

He had to be the third-base coach—why else would he be standing there? But he wasn't *my* third-base coach. In fact, I'd never seen *this* guy before either.

What was happening? Who were these people? Was I seeing things because of my knock on the head? Was I going nuts?

I started to get a really weird feeling. . . .

I licked my lips. "Sanders," I corrected him. "My name is Sanders. Uh—who are you?"

The man laughed. "That's our Buddy. Always kidding around."

"Quit gabbing and get your head in the game," the man with the shiny hair called from across the field.

He had to be the head coach. But why didn't I recognize him?

I peered at the next batter—*another* person I didn't know. In fact, I couldn't find a single familiar face on the whole field—or in either of the dugouts. Eve, Scott, Glen—they had all disappeared!

It was the same with the people in the bleachers. Total strangers, all of them. And they all wore funny clothes. For example, there wasn't a woman there without a funny-looking hat on. And they all wore gloves. In the middle of the summer!

And where were my parents? They had been in the stands five minutes ago. But now I couldn't spot them anywhere.

The pitcher zoomed a fastball down the center of the plate. The guy at bat took a huge cut at it. He crushed the ball, sending it sailing out of the park.

"Home run!" people screamed.

"What's the matter with you, Gibson? Don't just stand there. Run home," the third-base coach urged.

I ran to home plate. Then I trotted to the dugout. As I passed the fence, I caught a glimpse of the parking lot.

Whoa. A huge maroon car with an odd, rounded shape sat next to a pickup truck. The car looked as if it came from one of those old gangster movies. The truck was straight out of the *Beverly Hillbillies* reruns I sometimes watch.

"Uh—are we sharing the park with a classic car

27

show today?" I asked a freckle-faced kid in the dugout.

He stared at me as if I were crazy.

"What's a classic car?" he asked.

I started to feel more than weird. I started to feel downright scared.

I could think of only one explanation for all this.

I *was* crazy. The knock on the head had made me go insane.

My temples throbbed. I sat on the bench and rubbed my head. My hair felt funny somehow. Stiff.

"Are you okay, Buddy? You don't look so hot," the freckle-faced kid told me.

I'm not okay! I wanted to shout. I'm going nuts!

But I was scared to say it out loud. What would they do to me if I were crazy? Take me off to a nuthouse?

"Head hurts," I mumbled at last.

I glanced down to the end of the dugout. A dozen strange, small gloves lay in a pile on the ground. They looked like pot holders. Leather pot holders. Not baseball mitts.

Nearby was a stack of wooden bats.

Wooden bats? Our league always used aluminum bats. Didn't we?

I was still trying to figure it all out, when the freckled kid poked me with a bat. "Get up, Buddy. Three outs."

"What?" I glanced up. Players in pin-striped uniforms streamed past me to the pile of gloves. It was our turn in the field.

I must have looked uncertain, because the man with the slicked-back hair reached into the pile and pulled out a glove.

"Get out there, Gibson," he barked. "We don't have all day."

I caught the glove and pulled it on as I ran for third. It looked small on my hand, but it felt like a perfect fit. Someone had written "Gibson" on it in blue ink.

That name again. I knew it from somewhere, but where?

Then, suddenly, I remembered the old man from yesterday. Ernie Ames. The guy Eve thought was a ghost.

Gibson was the kid Ernie told me about. Buddy Gibson. The kid in the photograph.

The photograph from *1948*.

I stopped running and stood there with my mouth open.

Could it be? Was it even possible?

I suddenly began to have trouble breathing. There was something I had to check out. Right away.

I dashed off the field and into the parking lot. I ran to the big maroon car and peered into the sideview mirror.

A stranger stared back out at me.

A stranger who had a blond crew cut instead of curly brown hair. Who had blue eyes, not brown. Who had a small scar over his right eyebrow. Who was about four inches taller than me.

A stranger who looked just like the kid in that 1948 photo.

The world seemed to swoop in a dizzy circle around me.

Now it was all starting to make sense—in a horrible way.

Now I understood why all the uniforms looked so goofy. Why the gloves were weird. Why everything seemed as if it had come from an antique shop.

And why everyone kept calling me Gibson.

Somehow, I *was* Gibson.

Somehow, I had gone back in time!

7

I stood there, stunned.

I had gone back in time!

Back—into someone else's body!

How? How did it happen?

I was broken out of my daze by the coach with the slicked-back hair. He ran over to me and grabbed my arm. "What is the matter with you, Gibson? Are you nuts?" he demanded. "Get out on that field. Now!"

He hustled me back to the diamond. I stumbled toward third base.

Think, I told myself. I just have to think.

"Hey, what inning is it?" I asked the catcher as I passed home plate.

"The ninth." He grinned. "Looks like another winner!"

I couldn't concentrate on the game at all. My mind kept whirling, trying to figure out what had happened. And how.

I rubbed the side of my head through my cap. There was still a little pain.

Was that it? I wondered. Could my knock on the head have made me *believe* I went back in time? Could it have made me see Buddy Gibson's face in the mirror instead of mine?

I nearly blew an easy play, when a line drive popped out of my tiny glove. But I scrambled to pick it up and managed to make the throw to first in time.

The left fielder hollered at me. "What's the matter, Gibson? Can't handle a little pepper?"

I glared back at him. He was tremendous—he looked closer to fourteen than twelve. He had reddish hair and a mean squint. I thought he might make a better linebacker than a fielder.

Normally, I would have answered him. But I kept my mouth shut. I didn't want to talk to anyone until I was sure of what was going on.

"Play ball!" the umpire shouted.

As the inning went on, I studied the people around me. Under their ball caps, most of the guys wore buzz cuts.

Most of *my* teammates, back in real time, had longer hair.

And my shoes. They were heavy, clunky, spiked things, stiff as iron. Nothing like my Nikes.

I *must* have gone back in time. Everything seemed so real. The nerdy-looking uniforms. The gloves.

Even the name "Gibson" written on my glove. The "S" was a little lopsided by the glove's seam. I couldn't *imagine* things in so much detail—could I?

I thought about Ernie. I played back our conversation in my mind, trying to remember everything he said about Gibson. And about 1948.

He said they called this team the Doom Squad. Because everyone that played them was doomed to lose.

And because—

I caught my breath, remembering the old man's words. "Now they're buried in the Fear Street Cemetery!"

They all died after the championship game!

I sucked in my breath. Holy cow! Was *this* the championship game?

I peered over my shoulder at the scoreboard in right field.

Shadyside, seven. Oneiga, two. We were up five runs in the ninth inning.

Ernie told me that in the championship game Shadyside was ahead by only two in the ninth.

Whew! It must be a different game. I was safe—for now.

But I had to get out of here before that game!

Then my mind flashed to another part of my

33

conversation with Ernie. My wish. I told him I wanted to play on the best Shadyside team ever.

Was that it?

Was my wish coming true?

"Strike three. You're out!" the umpire bellowed.

Three outs. The game was over. We won.

But it wasn't a victory I could enjoy.

As we were jogging in, the big left fielder pumped a fist in the air. "That's what you get when you play the Doom Squad, boys. A big 'L' in the score book. We are your doom!"

Doom. I shuddered at the word.

I *really* had to get out of here!

Then I thought of something. If I landed in the past because of a wish, maybe a wish would get me back to my own time!

I had to try. Outside the dugout, I tossed my glove down and shut my eyes tight. I balled my hands into fists.

I want to go home! I screamed in my mind. I want to go home!

"Okay, boys. Gather 'round," a voice called.

I opened one eye. Then the other.

The first thing I saw was the coach with the slicked-back hair.

I groaned. It was still 1948.

Everyone on the team gathered around. I joined them.

The coach stood with his hands in his jacket pockets. A cigarette dangled from his lips. Gross.

"Okay, guys, good job today," the coach said. "Keep playing like this, and we're on our way to the trophy for sure. We're just one game away. We'll be the champions of 1948! Let's hear it!"

"Yeah!" everybody cheered. Guys pounded me on the back.

I just stood there and tried to smile.

The players gathered their stuff. We crossed the parking lot to the bus. Everybody chattered away, laughing and happy.

Except me. I was miserable.

How was I going to get back to my own time?

I stood in line, waiting to board the bus. When I climbed the steps, I stopped in shock.

Behind the steering wheel sat the old man from the house on Fear Street! Ernie Ames!

He was here with me in the past!

My heart jumped in my chest.

If he made it to the past—maybe he could bring me back to the future.

Maybe.

8

"**I**t's you!" I cried. I lunged at Ernie and grabbed him by the collar of his jacket. "I didn't mean it. Take me back. Take me back home. I don't want to be stuck here! Please!"

"Well, if you get out of everybody's way and let go of me, I'll be happy to take you back." The old man gave me a friendly smile.

"Really?" I gasped. "You will?"

Ernie laughed. "I'm the bus driver, Buddy. That's my job."

"No, I mean send me to the future. You can do it—can't you?"

Ernie's smile faded. I saw him shift his gaze to someone behind me.

The coach clapped a hand on my shoulder.

"Buddy took a knock today, Ernie," he told the bus driver. He pointed to his head. "Fastball right to the old noggin."

The bus driver nodded knowingly.

"Come on, Buddy. This way," the coach ordered, steering me away from the driver. He frowned down at me. "Maybe we better have a doctor check you out when we get home."

I grasped the coach's arm. "Please, you have to believe me! I'm not Buddy Gibson!"

The coach's frown deepened.

"I'm not!" I insisted. "I'm Buddy *Sanders*. And I'm from the future. I live in 1997!"

"Oh! So that's what this is." Coach grinned at me. "Sure, Buddy. You're from the future. And I'm the Lone Ranger. I'm just riding this bus until Silver comes along. He's my wonder horse, you know."

Laughter rang out all around me. Everyone on the team cracked up like this was some kind of joke.

I sighed, realizing the truth. No one believed me.

I turned and let the coach lead me to a seat. Why *should* they believe me? I thought. I sound completely crazy.

Coach stopped at a seat and pointed. "There you go, Buddy. And there's your book, right where you left it."

I glanced down. A novel lay on the seat. *Tom Swift and the Amazing Time Machine.*

"You and your science fiction," Coach grumbled. "I

37

don't know why you like that stuff so much. It'll rot your brain."

He picked up the book and leafed through the pages. "Where were you from last week? Mars, right?"

A short, sandy-haired kid with big buck teeth plopped into the seat next to me. "Yeah," he said. "Buddy was John Carter from Mars." He laughed.

The coach scanned the rows of seats. Then he walked up to the front. "Okay, Ernie. Everyone's here. Let's head out."

The bus jerked into motion. We pulled away from the Oneiga ball field.

"That Buddy's got some imagination," I heard the coach say to Ernie, the driver. "What a joker!"

This was awful. Not only did no one believe me—they didn't even think I was acting unusual. This Gibson kid made things up all the time.

We made a left turn at the end of the street and pulled onto a two-lane road. I stared out the window—we should be getting on the interstate! A six-lane highway! What happened to it?

I slouched back in my seat. It's 1948, I reminded myself. The interstate isn't even built yet.

Two seats in front of me, the big, ugly left fielder stood up. "Hey, guys, check this out," he called.

He pointed his arms straight out in front of him. "I am Buddy Gibson," he said in a robot voice. "I am from the future."

The kids sitting around him burst out laughing.

I glanced at the kid next to me. His face was covered with dark freckles. His big buck teeth stuck out even farther when he grinned at the fielder's joke. But at least he didn't laugh.

"What's your name?" I asked him.

"Don't play with me, Buddy. You've only known me your whole life." Then he frowned. "Say, how hard did that ball hit you?"

"Pretty hard," I told him. I leaned over and whispered, "I think maybe I have a little—what do you call it? Oh, yeah, amnesia."

The kid's eyes widened and he grinned. "Whoa! No kidding? That's neato!"

Neato?

Nerd-o! I thought.

"So—who are you?" I asked again.

"Johnny Beans. Center field. Remember?"

"Oh, yeah. Now I remember," I said. I wasn't lying. I *did* remember the kid—from the photograph the old man on Fear Street showed me.

"Who's the big doofus?" I pointed to the left fielder.

"That's Boog. Boog Johnson."

"He doesn't like me much, does he?" I asked.

"No, I guess he doesn't," Johnny agreed. "In fact, he doesn't like you—period."

Boog turned in his seat. He smirked at me. "Hey,

39

what's the news, future man? Who's going to win the World Series this year?"

Actually, I knew the answer to that. It was in one of my baseball books. The Cleveland Indians won in 1948. They beat Boston.

But I wasn't going to tell this jerk about it!

Boog stretched out his arms to either side. He ran up and down the aisle of the bus. "Get me. I'm Gibson in my very own space rocket. Zoom! Zoom!"

"Knock it off back there," the coach yelled. "No running around on the bus!"

Boog slinked back to his seat. He shot me a dirty look—as if it were my fault he got in trouble.

Turning my shoulder to Boog, I asked Johnny some more questions. He identified everyone on the bus for me. I sat back and pretended that it was all coming back to me.

As Johnny talked, I stared hard at the back of Ernie's head. Did he recognize me? Did he remember our meeting on Fear Street? I couldn't tell.

But he had to be the key to why I was here.

Maybe he did know who I was, but he didn't want to say so in front of all these people.

I had to find a way to talk to him when no one else was around.

I stared out the window, watching trees and buildings whiz by. Yes, I decided. That was—

I suddenly heard the sound of squealing brakes.

The bus shuddered to a stop. I pitched forward, banging my chin on the seat in front of me.

"Oof!" "Ow!" "Hey, watch it!" I heard my teammates holler.

"Sorry, guys," Ernie called back to us. "That truck in front of us skidded. We almost slammed into it. It was pretty close, but we're okay."

The accident! I thought. Sure, we're okay now. But soon a big old train really *will* slam into this bus! And if I don't do something, I'll be *in* the bus when it does!

No way. I had to get back to my own time before the train wreck happened. Before the championship game.

I turned to Johnny Beans.

"Tell me again. How many more games before the championship?"

Beans grinned. "Just one. Then we take the championship—and the trophy will be ours. Best in the state!"

It sounded great. But I knew the truth.

The Shadyside team wasn't going to win the championship game. They were doomed.

And if I didn't think of something fast—so was I!

9

The bus pulled into town on Village Road. I stared out the window. Would I recognize Shadyside in 1948?

We passed the fire department. And the police station. They both seemed pretty much the same.

But when I looked to my left, my mouth dropped open. Division Street Mall was gone! Or I guess it wasn't there yet. Neither was the ten-plex movie theater. Dalby's Department Store stood all by itself on the corner.

Across the street, the bowling alley stood as always, but a sign hung from it saying GRAND OPENING. Where the Rollerblading rink should have been, there was only an empty lot.

The bus continued along Village Road until we

reached the parking lot of Shadyside Middle School. I recognized the red brick building, even though the sign said SHADYSIDE JUNIOR HIGH SCHOOL.

Coach stood up at the front of the bus. "Okay, boys. We have one game before the championship. And I don't just want to beat this last team. I want to *destroy* them!"

"Yeah!" everybody yelled.

"I want them shaking in their shoes when we run out on that field!"

"Yeah!" the team replied.

"And why?"

"Because we're the Doom Squad!" the team roared.

"You bet we are." Coach nodded, looking satisfied.

Wow. My coach—my *real* coach, back in 1997— never talked like that. He said stuff like "Just remember, we're all out here to have fun."

Weird.

Coach put a hand on my arm as I was climbing off the bus. "How's the head, Buddy?" he asked. "Feeling better?"

"Yeah, Coach. I'm fine." I answered quickly.

I didn't want anyone to send me to a doctor. Who knows what medicine was like in 1948? What if they still used leeches to suck your blood or something?

"Glad to hear it," Coach said, smiling. "We can't afford to lose you. We might manage with somebody else hurt, but you're the star. We need you."

Out of the corner of my eye I saw Boog Johnson glaring at me. What was his problem?

As he walked past me, he leaned close to my ear and growled, "You think you're so hot."

"Forget him. He's just jealous," Johnny Beans whispered.

"I'd like to forget him, but I think he's going to pound me!" I said, worried.

"He wishes. I don't think he'd dare. Not until after the season anyway. His dad would kill him."

I started to walk toward my house on Spring Street. Then I remembered.

In 1948 I didn't live on Spring Street.

I wasn't even born yet.

My *parents* weren't even born yet!

I turned back to Johnny Beans. "Uh, I forgot where I live," I mumbled.

He shook his head. "Jeez, Louise, you *do* have amnesia!"

Jeez Louise? Man, these guys talked weird.

"Don't you remember?" Johnny continued. "Your house used to be in North Hills, but your folks moved last month. Now you're staying with Coach Johnson until the season's over."

"Oh—thanks," I said.

"Let's go, Gibson," someone shouted.

I turned and saw Coach standing by a humongous blue car. He waved at me. Boog stood next to him.

"Get a move on. I'm hungry," Boog bellowed.

I trotted over. Coach must be giving Boog a ride home.

Boog opened the front door.

"You get in back, son," the coach ordered. "Let Buddy ride up front with me."

Son?

That's when it hit me. Boog *Johnson?* Coach *Johnson?*

I groaned. I couldn't believe it! I was staying at the coach's house—that meant I was staying with Boog. The kid who wanted to pound me.

Great. Just great.

I climbed in and tried not to notice the stare Boog gave me.

I tugged hard on the heavy door to get it shut. Then I settled into the seat. Whoa! The coach's car was built like a tank!

Whoops! Have to buckle up, I thought. I dug around in the seat cushions.

"What are you doing?" Coach Johnson asked.

"I'm looking for my seat belt."

"Seat belt? What's a seat belt?" Boog scowled at me from the back.

Uh-oh . . . 1948 again. Maybe they didn't have seat belts in those days! "Heh-heh. Just joking," I mumbled.

"Seat belts," the coach snorted. "I've read about

45

them. Death traps, that's what they are. No, sir. I'm not letting anybody strap *me* into a car so I can't get away."

We drove out of the school parking lot and headed down Hawthorne Drive. We made a right turn on Park.

Then the coach turned right again—on Fear Street.

I should have guessed that's where Boog would live.

We cruised up the street, then turned left into the drive of a rambling two-story house. I got out of the car and glanced across the street.

A familiar-looking house stared back at me. Then I realized how I knew it. It was the house from my own time. The house where I met Ernie Ames, the bus driver.

The house where everything started.

Only now it didn't look abandoned. It was a little shabby, maybe, but the paint wasn't peeling off or anything.

An old car pulled into the house's driveway. The engine died and the bus driver stepped out.

He waved to me. I waved back slowly.

Did he recognize me? I mean *me*, Buddy Sanders?

I've got to talk to him, I thought. Alone. I need to find out why he sent me here—and how I'm supposed to get back to my own time.

"Buddy," Coach Johnson called. "Come on inside."

"Sure," I said. I walked slowly toward the John-sons' house.

Everything is going to be okay, I told myself. All I have to do is stay calm.

Calm—hah! If I knew then what was about to happen to me, I would have run screaming down Fear Street.

Because my nightmare was just starting!

10

━━━━◆━━━━

We tromped up the wooden steps to the front door.
A lady who had to be Boog's mom stood in the
doorway, waiting for us.

Her red hair hung to her shoulders, and her cheeks
had a rosy glow. She wore a dark blue dress with a
white lace collar.

"Don't take another step without taking those
muddy shoes off! I just scrubbed these floors," she
scolded. Then she smiled. "So, how did we do today,
boys?"

"A feast for your conquering heroes!" Coach Johnson teased.

Mrs. Johnson laughed. "I guess you won again."

"Don't we always, Mom?" Boog asked.

"It was a close call though," the coach said. "We almost lost our star player to a fastball to his head."

Mrs. Johnson gasped. "Oh, no! Here, Buddy, let me see." She tipped my head to the side and probed gently at the bruise. She made a soft "tsk."

"It looks painful," she told me. "But I think you'll live. Not a lot of swelling. Any dizziness, Buddy? Are you feeling sleepy?"

"I'm okay," I mumbled.

"Good. Now, you boys run upstairs and wash up for supper. Everything's ready. Go on, scoot."

I followed Boog up the stairs, thinking that people were sure a lot less careful in 1948. In my own time, Mom and Dad would have sent me to the doctor as soon as I was hit.

I stopped at the top of the stairs and looked around, confused. Boog stood in a doorway. "Well? You just going to stand there?" he snapped.

"I don't remember—"

Boog's eyes narrowed. "What's with you, Buddy?" He pointed to a door down the hall. "In there. I got dibs on the bathroom."

He stepped into the bathroom and slammed the door. I heard water running. Good. He was out of my way. Now I could really check the place out.

I went down the hall and opened the door to the room Buddy Gibson was staying in. It was smaller than the one I had at home, but it looked nice and cozy. It had a shelf filled with Hardy Boys and Tarzan books. Hey! I read those—way in the future. Gibson had a few of those Tom Swift books too.

I looked around for the stereo. It was nowhere to be found.

Maybe he's got a TV, I thought. But I couldn't find one of those either.

Duh—1948. Hardly anyone had TVs back then.

So what did people do for fun around here?

I spied a window at the far end of the room. I walked over to it and lifted the blinds.

Yes! The window faced the front. I could see Fear Street, and Ernie the bus driver's house.

I glanced down. A rose trellis clung to the side of the house—right below the window. Perfect for climbing out after dark. All right!

Someone knocked on the door. I dropped the blinds.

"I'm done in the bathroom. You're up, goofus," Boog bellowed from the other side.

"Keep your shirt on, you big loser," I muttered under my breath.

There was a chest of drawers positioned against the wall behind me. A mirror was placed over it.

I stooped to open one of the drawers, and caught my reflection in the mirror. There it was again. Buddy Gibson's face, with the blue eyes and the scar. I shuddered.

Looking like someone else—*being* someone else—

was the creepiest part about this whole nightmare. A guy just doesn't expect to see someone else in the mirror.

I opened one of the dresser drawers. Inside I found shirts and pants, neatly folded and sorted. The shirts were all plaid. That wouldn't have been so bad if they were flannel. But they weren't. They were this scratchy cotton material. They had short sleeves and narrow collars.

The pants were mostly jeans. Stiff, dark blue jeans that looked like they could stand up all by themselves.

I changed into fresh clothes, then glanced in the mirror again. Geek city! I wouldn't be caught dead in these clothes back home.

But this was 1948. I'd probably blend right in with all the other nerds here.

The door opened again, and Boog came in. "Come on, supper's waiting." He jabbed at me with his fist. I jerked backward.

"Hah! Flinch!" he said, and grabbed my arm. "Frog!" Then he hit me hard in the muscle of my left arm.

"Ow!" I cried. "Hey, that hurt." I made a fist.

When Boog saw it, his lips curled in a mean smile.

"You flinched, tough guy," he reminded me. "So I get to frog you. That's the rule, and you know it. Or are you too big a sissy to trade licks?"

He sneered and pushed me backward. "Huh?" he challenged. He shoved me again. "How about it? You

51

too much of a baby? Or maybe you want to go outside and fight for real?" He shoved me again.

I had just about had enough of this guy. He was big. But I didn't care. Nobody pushes me around like that.

"Quit it!" I shouted. I shoved him back—hard— and caught him by surprise. He stumbled backward and tripped on the rug. He landed with a crash. Right on his rear end.

He picked himself up. "Now you're going to get it!" he snarled.

I'd studied karate for two months when I was eleven. I took a stance, just like my instructor showed me.

Boog didn't know it, but I was about to become the Karate Kid.

Then Boog stood up to his full height.

Uh-oh, I thought. He's really big, isn't he?

And he looks really strong.

Boog came at me with his fist cocked back.

Yikes! I thought. Here it comes!

And then he swung—straight at my face.

Boog's fist drove toward my face.

I gritted my teeth.

Then Coach Johnson's voice roared up the stairs.

"Knock off the roughhousing, you two. You sound like a herd of elephants up there!"

Boog's fist stopped—an inch from my nose. He grinned at me.

"You got lucky, Gibson. But next time I'm going to pulverize you."

"Yeah, sure," I said. I rubbed the sore place on my arm and glared at him. No way would I let him know I was scared.

But I was.

Boog went out of the room first. I stayed behind a second to calm down. And think.

Being trapped in the past was bad enough. But now I had another problem. Boog.

I had to get out of there before he pulverized me.

I had to talk to Ernie. Tonight!

Dinner was incredible. Thick slabs of roast beef. Gravy. Mashed potatoes. Peas glistening with butter. Creamed corn. Slices of white bread smeared with *more* butter. Peach cobbler with cream for dessert.

My mom cooks "heart-healthy" food. I think she would have fainted at the sight of all that fat.

It tasted great. But by the time I worked through my second helping of cobbler, I was worried that I might burst.

Did they eat like this every day?

After dinner everyone sat in the living room and listened to the radio. Some guy named Fred Allen. The Johnsons all thought he was a riot. I couldn't figure out what was so funny myself. Another thing that changed since 1948, I guess.

I sat around with them as long as I could stand it. Then I stood up and stretched. "I think I'll go to bed," I announced.

Boog curled his lip. "What are you, a baby? It's only a quarter to nine."

"Buddy needs his rest," Coach Johnson snapped. "Especially after that knock on the head. You go along, Buddy."

I didn't miss the dirty look Boog shot me.

I wished his dad had kept quiet. He was trying to help, I guess. But really, he made Boog hate me even more.

I trudged up the stairs and into my room. Standing by the door, I listened for a moment. Good. They were all still laughing away at Fred Allen.

Time to pay a visit to the bus driver.

The window in my room was already open wide. I swung my legs over the sill. Then I let myself down until I dangled by my hands. I grasped the wooden rose trellis and began to climb.

"Ow. Ouch!" I muttered under my breath. Thorns pricked through my plaid shirt and into my skin.

When I reached the bottom, I crept across the lawn to the Johnsons' hedge. I peered over its leafy top at the bus driver's house.

The lights on the first floor were still on. They cast a faint light over his overgrown lawn. It was a good thing, because all the streetlamps on the block were out.

Just one more cheerful detail about Fear Street.

I stole across Fear Street. I made my way up to the bus driver's rickety porch. I climbed up to the door and knocked softly.

Ernie opened the door. "Buddy! What are you doing here?" He smiled. "This is a nice surprise. I don't get a lot of visitors. Come on in."

He didn't have to ask me twice. I barreled past him into the house.

He closed the door. "Would you like a soda pop, or—"

"Listen," I interrupted. "I don't know why you sent me back here—or how. But this is not what I wished for—understand? I want to go home. You have to send me back!"

Ernie's eyebrows drew together. "Take it easy, Buddy. What are you talking about?"

"I know you remember me," I insisted. The words tumbled out of my mouth. "I'm Buddy *Sanders*—not Buddy Gibson. I'm from the future. You sent me here because of my wish. Because I wished to be on the best team ever. But I wanted *my* team to be the best team ever. I didn't want to be here!"

A strange look crossed Ernie's face. "All right, Buddy," he said in a soothing voice. "You want me to send you back? I'll send you back. No problem."

"You—you will?" I stared at him. I didn't think it would be so easy.

"Just wait right there," Ernie instructed. "I—uh— I have to get the time machine ready." He shuffled out of the room, pulling the door closed behind him.

Time machine? I never thought of that. It never occurred to me that I was brought here by a machine. But I guessed it made sense. How else could Ernie move people back and forth?

Then in the other room I heard Ernie's voice. He spoke softly. Who was he talking to? I thought he lived alone.

56

I walked over to the door he went through. It was open a crack. His voice drifted through.

"Get me the Johnson house, Eunice. . . . Yeah, I know it's right across the street from me, but this is an emergency!"

Wait a minute. What was he doing?

"Hello, Mr. Johnson?" Ernie whispered. "I think you'd better come over here right away. Buddy's here." He paused. "How should I know how he got here? All I know is, he's here, and he's talking crazy. Saying he wants me to send him back to the future. And believe me—he's not kidding. That fastball did more damage than you think!"

Oh, no! I realized. Ernie thinks I'm *nuts!*

I had to get out of there—fast. Or they would stick me in some hospital for sure.

I didn't want to go to a hospital. I just wanted to get back home—to my own time.

I raced to Ernie's front door and threw it open.

Coach Johnson strode up the walk outside.

"No!" I gasped. I tore into Ernie's kitchen. I knew there was a back door in there—I remembered Ernie using it when I met him the first time.

There! I darted over and slid the bolt.

Then I ran into the night. Through Ernie's backyard. Around the side of his house. And down Fear Street—in the dark.

Coach Johnson's voice rang out behind me. "Buddy! Stop!"

I sprinted down the street. Heavy steps pounded after me.

I had no idea where I was going. I just ran.

Then, directly in front of me, I saw a patch of deeper darkness. It was just . . . black. Like the deepest shadow on a bright, sunny day.

It lay across my path. A wave of cold washed toward me.

The hair rose on the back of my neck.

I didn't even slow down. I just veered to my left. I ran toward a tall iron gate. Through it I glimpsed shadowy trees and a lot of whitish rocks. Maybe I could hide in there.

It wasn't until I passed through the gates that I began to guess where I was. The white rocks—why did they all have the same shape? Sort of rectangular, with rounded tops.

Uh-oh.

They weren't plain old rocks.

They were gravestones.

I was in the Fear Street Cemetery!

12

The Fear Street Cemetery!

My skin crawled. I wasn't about to hide in *there*. I had to find a way out!

I slowed to a jog, peering right and left.

"Buddy!" Coach Johnson called again. "Where are you going? Come back!"

His voice sounded close. I risked a glance over my shoulder.

The next thing I knew, I was flying through the air. I must have caught my foot on a root or something.

I whacked my head hard on a low branch.

Then I hit the ground.

And everything went black.

* * *

When I opened my eyes again, the first thing I saw was Mrs. Johnson's worried face. She bent over me, biting her lip.

I couldn't help groaning. And not just because my head was killing me.

I was right back where I started! At the Johnsons' house. In Buddy Gibson's bedroom.

Another face came into view. A silver-haired man with a white coat. He peered deep into my eyes as I lay in bed. "Can you hear me, son?"

"Yes," I mumbled.

"What's your name?" he asked.

"Buddy. My name is Buddy."

"What's your last name?" he wanted to know.

There was no point telling the truth. I already found that out. Nobody believed me.

I gritted my teeth. "Gibson," I replied.

"Good, good. And what year is this?"

"It's 1948," I muttered.

Then the doctor shined a light in my eyes and asked me to follow his finger as he moved it around. I did what I was told.

The doctor straightened up. "He's all right," he told Mrs. Johnson. "No sign of concussion. And he doesn't seem confused anymore. My guess is, that second knock on the head knocked his wits back into order." He laughed.

I glared at him from my bed. I didn't think it was funny at all.

"Keep an eye on him for the next few days, and let me know if you notice any more strange behavior," the doctor advised. "But I think he'll be just fine."

"Thank you, Doctor." Mrs. Johnson breathed a sigh of relief. The doctor left the room.

Mrs. Johnson leaned down and touched me on the forehead. "You gave everyone quite a scare, Buddy," she told me. Then she smiled. "But you're okay now. Try to get some rest."

"I'll try. Sorry for all the trouble, Mrs. Johnson," I said, closing my eyes.

She snapped off my lamp and went out. I lay there in the dark, thinking.

What went wrong with Ernie? He definitely didn't know what I was talking about. Did that mean he wasn't the one who brought me to the past?

Then I thought of an explanation that made my skin prickle.

There was a good reason Ernie didn't know what I was talking about. To him, the bus crash was still in the future. How could he know about something that hadn't happened yet?

That meant the Ernie that I met in my own time— the one who asked me what my wish was—really was a ghost. Eve was right.

I swallowed hard. So a ghost sent me into the past. But why? Why?

The question echoed in my brain until I finally fell asleep.

I don't know how much time went by. It felt like only a second passed before I was jerked awake. I lay in bed, listening.

What woke me?

I shivered. The room was strangely cold—even though it was the middle of summer. I gathered the sheet tighter around me.

I glanced at the alarm clock. With the moonlight from the window I could just make out the time. Three in the morning.

I swept my eyes around the room. Everything seemed normal, but the hairs on the back of my neck bristled. I had a feeling there was someone else there. Even though I could see no one.

A shadow moved across from me.

I sat up in bed. My heart thudded. "Boog? Is that you?" I demanded.

No answer.

"This isn't funny, man." I tried to keep my voice steady.

Still no answer. But the shadow seemed to drift in front of the window. The moonlight suddenly grew dimmer.

I strained my eyes in the darkness. All I could see was—black. Like the patch of inky shadow I saw on Fear Street earlier that night.

"Wh-who's there?" I stammered.

The darkness seemed to stretch toward me.

"You! Why did you do this to me?" a thin, cold voice whispered.

No way was that Boog's voice! Chills raced down my back.

"Who—who are you?" I croaked.

The shadow moved closer. It looked like a cloud of thick black smoke—with burning white holes for eyes!

Was it a ghost?

It loomed right in front of my face. "You'll pay!"

"Wh-what did I do? What do you want?" I managed to ask.

No answer. The shadow bulged toward me.

I shrank back. Numbing cold seeped into my bones.

Then the thing was on top of me. Covering my face. Pressing me down.

"Help!" I tried to shout. But I couldn't make a sound.

I couldn't breathe!

The shadow was crushing me!

13

I was being smothered—by a shadow!

I gasped and strained for air. Fingers of cold dug deep into my veins. It felt as though my blood was turning to ice.

I pushed against the shadow.

My hands passed right through it!

The horrible cold weight was crushing the air right out of my lungs. And I couldn't even touch it!

I grasped desperately at the thing. But my fingers closed on nothing.

This is it, I thought. I'm finished!

Then, suddenly, I could breathe again.

No more horrible weight on my chest.

No more icy chill.

I was struggling with my own sheets.

I peered around the room. My breath rasped loudly in the stillness. Moonlight poured in through the open window.

I lay there, shaking. Was it a dream? A horrible nightmare?

Then a ghostly voice whispered in my ear.

"I'll be back," it said. "I'm coming for you. And next time I'll be stronger."

I gasped. No dream. It was no dream!

A ghost attacked me!

A ghost from the Fear Street Cemetery.

Okay. I was ready to admit it.

"I believe in ghosts," I whispered.

But what did it want with me? What did *I* do to it? I didn't have a clue!

Gradually, the numbness bled from my veins. My breathing returned to normal.

My hand trembled as I flicked on the lamp. I swung my feet down to the floor and sat up. I glanced over at the mirror.

Buddy Gibson's square face stared back at me.

"Why?" I asked the reflection. "Why did you have to be living on Fear Street, of all places?"

Now things were even worse than before!

Not only did Boog want to pound me into the ground. Not only was I trapped in the past.

Now I had some crazy Fear Street ghost after me!

What was next? Plagues? Floods? Other natural disasters?

I remembered the ghost's words. It said it was getting stronger. And coming back.

What was I going to do?

There was only one answer. I had to get out of there before the thing came back.

But once again I had a basic problem: How?

Wishing didn't work. Neither did hitting my head again, the way I did in the cemetery. Not that I planned that!

And I knew now that Ernie wasn't going to help me. He didn't even know what I was talking about.

"Use your brain, Buddy," I told myself. "Think."

What did I know about time travel?

Not much! Until yesterday I never even believed it was possible.

I thought of all the TV shows I'd seen with time travel in them. In most cases, people traveled through time on purpose.

But then I remembered this one show where the guy couldn't control his travel. Like me.

In the show he could move on only if he changed history for the person whose body he was stuck in.

I thought about that. Change history.

Maybe *I* was supposed to change history!

But change *what*?

Then I slapped my forehead. Of course. The answer was obvious!

"The bus crash!" I said aloud.

Maybe I was supposed to save Gibson and his teammates from dying!

Maybe I was supposed to be a hero!

Cool.

But how could I do it?

Hmmm. Maybe if we lost our last game—tomorrow's game.

Yeah! I thought. That's it!

I paced around the room, excited. "If I throw the game—if I make Shadyside lose—the team won't make the championships," I whispered. "Then they won't be on that bus when the train comes by. Everyone would be saved!"

And maybe *I* would get to go back to my time.

The more I thought about it, the more it made sense. I was supposed to change history. That had to be it.

Okay. It was up to me to see we never played that championship game. One game to go, and all I had to do was make sure we lost it.

I hated the idea of throwing a game. Whenever I played baseball, I played to win. But really, what was more important—playing your best, or saving about twenty lives?

The answer was obvious. I knew what I had to do. Tomorrow the Shadyside team would be playing a crucial game.

And their big star, Buddy Gibson, would be doing his very best—to lose!

14

The next day was cloudy and muggy. I broke a sweat just getting out of bed. Why didn't someone turn on the air-conditioning?

Oh, yeah, 1948. No air-conditioning.

Still, the rotten weather had its good points. I lifted the blinds on the bedroom window and cheered on the clouds.

"Come on, guys. Rain us out," I whispered.

If we didn't play the game tonight, it would have to be played tomorrow. When we were supposed to be at the championships. History would change!

Then I remembered. In the past this game wasn't called because of rain. Shadyside played as scheduled. The weather was going to clear up—whether I liked it or not.

I sighed and went down to the kitchen. I began looking through the cabinets for some cereal or a Pop-Tart.

Mrs. Johnson pushed through the swinging doors from the dining room. "Buddy!" she cried. "How are you feeling?" She held me by the shoulders, studying my face. Her blue eyes were full of concern.

She was a nice lady. I felt bad for worrying her.

"I'm fine. Really," I answered. "Sorry I scared you yesterday. I—uh—I guess I was a little confused."

"Don't give it another thought, dear," Mrs. Johnson told me. "Go on into the dining room. Your breakfast is waiting."

I slid into a seat in the dining room. The table was covered with platters of pancakes, bacon, eggs, and potatoes. Boog sat there with a full plate, chowing down.

"Wow," I muttered under my breath. It was amazing to me these people could even move, they ate so much!

I loaded my plate with some pancakes and bacon. "Where's Coach?" I asked Boog.

He scowled at me. "At work, stupid."

While Boog and I ate, Mrs. Johnson fluttered around, dusting things. She wore a pink dress with a flowered apron tied over it.

I can't imagine *my* mom doing housework in a dress. She cleans in a grubby sweatshirt and a pair of old jeans.

I pushed my plate away and glanced at Boog. "What time is the game?" I asked.

"About three. Dad is leaving work early to make it there on time." He shoved one last giant forkful of eggs into his mouth and stood up. "Come on," he said. "Let's hit some flies and rollers."

"Okay," I agreed after a second.

I was surprised that Boog wanted to play ball with me. I hoped he wasn't just trying to get me alone so he could finish beating me up.

But I figured I might as well take the chance. It wasn't like I had anything else to do before the game.

The sun was already beaming through the clouds when we went outside. We crossed to Ernie's house and went through his backyard. Boog shoved aside the same fence boards I crawled through all those years in the future. We squirmed through the fence, into the same field where Eve and I practiced.

I mean, where we were *going* to practice, in fifty years.

Whatever. My brain was starting to hurt.

Boog's version of flies and rollers went like this: You catch five flies or ten ground balls to earn a turn at bat. Boog batted first, and man, did he make me work! He swatted balls all over the field. By the time I earned my chance at bat, I must have trotted two miles.

"Made you run," he snickered when he handed me the bat.

"Yeah, well, we'll see how you do, big guy," I puffed. I was so hot, I thought I might explode.

Boog hustled across the field, and I started hitting to him.

Anything I hit above his head, he could catch. No problem. But grounders and drives below the waist were hard for him.

After watching him for a minute, I waved him over. We ran and met about halfway.

"I think I know what you're doing wrong," I said.

Boog flushed. "Oh, yeah? I do all right, smart guy."

"Hey, chill out. I'm just trying to help."

"Chill out?" he sneered. "Where did you learn that dumb expression?"

"Uh, I—I heard it somewhere, I guess," I stammered. I had to watch what I said. *Chill out* was from way after Boog's time. "Anyway, I think I can help you with those low ones."

Boog folded his arms. "Is that so?"

Maybe this wasn't such a good idea, I thought. Boog was starting to look as if he wanted to pound me again. And anyway, the worse he played, the more chance we would have of losing the game today—and missing the championship.

"All right, genius, I'm waiting," Boog growled.

Me and my big mouth.

"See, it's natural to catch a high one," I began. "You put the glove between your eyes and the ball.

7 i

But for low ones, you put the glove between the ball and the ground, or the ball and your body. So you have to hold your head differently for those."

He looked slightly puzzled. "Yeah?"

"Yeah. Watch." I bent over and showed him what I meant, following the path of an imaginary ball.

He turned his glove, mimicking my moves.

Then, to my surprise, he grinned. "Hit me some."

He turned and chugged across the field. I trotted back to the fence and hit him a short fly ball, making him run up. He turned his glove at the last minute. The ball bounced off.

"Hold it like a basket for those," I yelled. "Open."

I hit him another. He got it that time. Then the next one, and the next, and the next.

By the time we finished, Boog was snagging everything I could hit. He ran up, grinning. "It works. Did you see that?" He pounded his fist in his glove. "Wait till Dad sees me now!"

I couldn't help grinning back at him. And it wasn't just because now he wouldn't try to beat me up anymore. It's corny, but I actually felt glad I helped Boog.

Boog pulled off his glove and shouldered the bat. "Come on, let's go see if Mom's got some lemonade."

We walked back to the fence. Boog crawled through. I glanced up and saw Ernie staring at us from an upstairs window.

The day suddenly seemed less bright. For a minute there, I had forgotten where I was. Playing ball, joking with Boog, made me relax.

But seeing Ernie reminded me of everything that happened the night before. The ghost, or whatever it was, that nearly smothered me in my bed.

I had to find a way to lose the game today. I had to get out of there *now*. If I didn't, it was going to take a lot more than lemonade to make me feel better.

Because that thing was coming back for me!

15

The game was played in Shadyside this time. No bus. We were the home team, so we took the field first. I stood at third and banged my fist into my glove. I was trying to beam mental messages to the batter.

Want to score some runs? I thought at him. Just hit it my way, and I'll see what I can do for you.

The first two batters struck out, but the third hit one my way I let it bounce off my glove. Then I chased after the ball as if I were in a hurry. I made sure I kicked it just as I reached to pick it up.

By the time I got the ball, the runner was on second. I decided to settle for that. If I made too many errors on one play, it would look suspicious.

"What is with you, Gibson?" Johnny Beans yelled. "You got holes in your glove or something?"

I shrugged my shoulders. "Sorry," I called back. I tried to sound as if I meant it.

The next batter walked. That meant the other team had runners on first and second, with two out.

The next batter kept fouling out to the left. I thought he might hit one down the third baseline, so I edged toward second.

Sure enough, he hit a bouncer right toward third base.

I made a big deal about diving for the ball. I knew I was short. It would go on by.

But then something weird happened.

The ball looked as if it struck an invisible wall in midair. It hung in the air for a split second.

Then it curved around and wobbled into my glove—without me doing a thing!

Huh?

I tried to miss it—but I caught it anyway!

"Nice play, Gibson!" Coach Johnson roared.

I climbed to my feet, staring at the ball in my glove.

The runner from second charged right into me for the third out.

The crowd in the bleachers cheered wildly as our team ran off the field. My teammates slapped me on the back and congratulated me. Even Boog called out, "Good one!"

"What a play!" Johnny Beans exclaimed as we tossed down our gloves. "How did you do that? I thought that ball was by you for sure!"

I shrugged. "Just a lucky break," I mumbled.

But it didn't *feel* like a lucky break. I was almost positive that ball changed course in midair.

Then a voice whispered behind me, "I know what you're doing, you rat. You're trying to lose! But I won't let you."

I whirled around.

No one behind me.

"Did—did you say something?" I asked Johnny.

"Nope," he replied.

But I knew that already.

Because I recognized that thin, cold voice. The voice from last night. From the ghost, or whatever it was, that attacked me.

It followed me! It was here!

And somehow it was interfering with the game!

Why? What did a ghost care about a baseball game? Why did a ghost want Shadyside to win?

In the dugout, I checked the lineup sheet. I was batting cleanup.

Good. I would make sure I struck out. There was nothing a ghost could do to prevent *that!*

The bases were loaded when I got to the plate. I stepped up with a hollow feeling in my stomach. I was never at bat before when I didn't try to do my best. But I made myself swing at the first two pitches like a goof.

My teammates yelled from the dugout.

"Use your eyes, Buddy."

"Don't swing at junk!"

"Come on, Gibson!"

I swung at the third pitch, a ball way outside. There was no way I could hit it.

Then the ball changed course.

Not like a curveball. It was as if the ball whacked into something and bounced off. It hit me on the elbow.

The umpire jumped up and hollered, "Hit by the pitch! Automatic walk. Take your base!"

I groaned and slung my bat toward the dugout. I trudged to first as the kid on third ambled home.

"Hah," the cold voice whispered in my ear. "You can't stop me. I'm growing stronger. I'm going to get you!"

I shuddered.

I was starting to realize the horrible truth.

I couldn't lose.

No matter what I did, the ghost wasn't going to let me throw the game. I didn't know why.

All I knew was, my chance to change history was going down the tubes.

And so was my chance to survive!

16

We won the game seven to three. Boog was a maniac in the outfield. He made one incredible play after another.

As for me, I kept trying my best to lose the game. But the harder I tried, the more I looked like a star.

My plays seemed impossible. The other guys started to stare at me as if I were some kind of wizard or something.

I couldn't blame them. The plays were totally impossible. The ghost made them all happen. I had nothing to do with it.

If I tripped over my own feet, something would make me sail gracefully through the air and snag a line drive like a Hall of Famer.

If I threw wide, the ball would curve like a Frisbee and smack solidly into the first baseman's glove.

If I hit a fly ball, it would just keep going—and going—until it soared over the fence and vanished.

I could have played standing on my head and never missed a lick.

It was horrible!

After the game, Coach Johnson drove Boog and me into town. He dropped us off at a little grocery store. "I've got to do some errands," he explained. "Why don't you boys get yourselves a few goodies? My treat." He reached into his pocket.

Excellent! I thought. I'd really love a can of soda right now. And maybe a candy bar.

Then coach handed each of us a quarter.

A quarter! I stared at the coin. What could I possibly get for twenty-five lousy cents?

"Thanks, Dad!" Boog said happily. "Let's go, Buddy."

I followed him into the tiny store. It was crammed with old-fashioned–looking cans and bottles, stacked on wooden shelves. Jars of hard candy lined the counter. Below them lay rows of candy bars and gum.

A big red cooler stood by the counter. COCA-COLA was written on the side. Boog walked over to it and opened the lid.

I peered inside and saw rows of bottles hanging from racks by their tops. Boog slid a Coke free. I watched closely and did what he did.

When I opened it, the drink was just a little bit frozen. It tasted really good. Even better than Coke usually tasted.

And the best part was, I bought the Coke, a bag of gum, and a Three Musketeers bar for only eleven cents! Also, the candy bar was definitely bigger than the ones in my own time.

I guess 1948 did have its good points.

Boog and I sat on a bench in front of the store. We ate our candy while we watched the cars go by.

Boog was obviously feeling good. "Did you hear what Dad told me?" he asked, trying to sound casual. "He said it was the best he'd ever seen me play."

"You had a great game," I agreed glumly.

"Not as good as yours though," Boog said generously. He drained his soda and belched. "I feel like I hit my stride today. I just wish the season wasn't almost over."

"I know. I wish it would go on too," I agreed.

Boy, did I wish!

But tomorrow was the championship. Do-or-die time.

No joke!

Boog leaned back on the bench and took a deep breath. "Just smell that summer air, Buddy. That's baseball air. And tomorrow will be the best day. We'll win the championship and everyone will know we're number one. Man, life is sweet."

His words made me feel miserable. The best day? Hardly. The *last* day was more like it. The *worst* day.

There had to be something more I could do to stop the accident!

I could run away, I thought. Then I could hide long enough to stay off that bus. To stay alive.

But what about everybody else on the team? What about Johnny Beans? And Boog?

Maybe I should try to tell Boog what I knew. Then he would know to stay off the bus too.

Forget it. He would just think I was crazy—like everyone else did. "Been there, done that," I muttered.

"What?" Boog asked.

"Nothing," I answered, sighing.

No. There was nothing I could do but run away. Save myself—and hope that I could find my way back to my own time someday. I couldn't worry about the rest of the team.

And then I got an idea.

It was so simple, I almost didn't believe it could work. But the more I thought about it, the more it made sense.

Yes!

A stupid grin crept across my face. "You know what?" I said.

"What?" Boog glanced at me.

"We *are* going to win that game tomorrow," I declared.

81

He laughed. "Sure we are!" He punched me on the shoulder. "We're the Doom Squad! We have to win!"

You are so right, I thought. We *have* to win!

If we win, we'll go to the party after the game. We won't get right on the bus to go home.

And we won't be on those tracks when the train comes to squash us.

And I know how to win the game! I know what the last play will be! Ernie told me about it before I ended up in the past.

All I have to do is hug the foul line and grab that last line drive. And I'll save the whole team!

I'll change history!

Butterflies fluttered in my stomach. Now that I knew what to do, I wondered if I could pull it off. Everything had to go just right. I had to play the best game of my life!

All I knew was, I'd *better* have what it takes.

Then I remembered my other little problem.

That ghost. It told me it was coming back. Coming for me.

Would I still be around for tomorrow's game?

17

That night, as I brushed my teeth in the bathroom, I got the feeling someone was watching me.

I stopped mid-brush. Toothpaste ran from my mouth. I glanced up into the mirror.

No one there.

After a second, I spat out the rest of the toothpaste and reached for the towel.

Wait—did I glimpse something in the mirror?

No. It was only me. Or, rather, Buddy Gibson. His face looked back at me from the mirror. It still freaked me out. That blond crew cut. The scar. They didn't belong to me!

Shivering, I turned away from the mirror. I went into my room and slid into bed. I switched off the lamp. Darkness surrounded me.

I listened to the sounds of the house settling down. I had to stay awake. I didn't want that ghost to catch me by surprise. Once I was sure the adults were in bed, I would switch the lamp back on.

But even though I was terrified, I was wiped out. After a while I drifted off.

When I opened my eyes again, it was hours later. I lay in bed, tense.

The last time I woke like this, I had a visitor.

I stared around. I saw nothing unusual.

Moonlight poured through the window. My desk chair cast a long shadow on the wall.

Very slowly I sat up, careful to make no sound. I studied the shadows.

Did this one move? Did that one?

"You're just working yourself up," I whispered.

But *something* woke me. I was sure of it.

And something was different about this room. What was it?

The closet door. It was closed. Wasn't it open when I went to bed?

Mrs. Johnson probably came in and shut it while I was asleep, I thought. That's all.

But I couldn't convince myself. The more I stared at the door, the more nervous I got.

I licked my lips. I felt my heart stepping up its rhythm. I had to do something before I scared myself to death.

I reached for the lamp switch and turned it.

The bulb blew out with a loud crackle.

"Great," I muttered. "Just great."

I eased out of bed and tiptoed to the door. I flipped the switch for the overhead light. I sighed with relief as light flooded the room.

The shadows vanished.

Now, with the light on, my fears felt foolish. Just my imagination running away with me. I took a deep breath, trying to calm my racing heart.

Now I could go back to bed.

Wait. Not just yet.

I had to see if there was anything behind the closet door.

I padded over to the closet and put my hand on the doorknob. I turned it.

CRACKKKKK!

The overhead bulb blew out.

I tried to slam the door shut. But it was too late. It swung open with a slow creak. I couldn't hold it closed.

I gasped. The moonlight fell across a figure in the closet. It was dark, smoky. It seemed wrapped in shadows. But this time I could make out features.

Human features. A head. A neck. A face.

I backed away from the closet. Cold sweat prickled on my forehead.

The ghost floated forward. Its arms rose and

reached for me. Now I could see its features more clearly. I felt as though I were looking at a photo negative. A walking negative—of a kid about my age.

I could make out a small nose. Glittering eyes. A hot white scar above one brow.

Wait.

I knew this kid!

"Gibson!" I whispered.

"That's right," the thing snarled. "It's me. The real Buddy Gibson. You stole my body from me. And I want it back!"

18

"**T**his can't be happening!" I moaned.

But it was. The glowing form of Buddy Gibson lurched toward me. I turned to run.

Something tripped me. I fell on my face.

"Give me my body back!" The ghostly voice was stronger than before.

I rolled over onto my back. Buddy Gibson loomed above me. He was easy to recognize now. He looked solid. Terrifyingly real.

He grabbed me by the collar of my pajamas and lifted me off the floor. He was so strong!

"Give it back," he snarled. "Give it back!"

"Please, Buddy. I don't know how this happened!" I tried to explain. "It wasn't me. I didn't do it."

"Liar! You're trying to trick me!" Gibson grinned nastily. "But it won't work."

He held out his hand. He reached toward my chest. Waves of cold flowed over me. He moved his hand closer.

It began to disappear.

It was sinking slowly into my chest!

"What are you doing?" I gasped in horror.

"It's my body!" Gibson cried. "I'm taking it back!"

Panicked, I shoved him with all my might. He must not have been ready for it. He stumbled backward to the floor.

So did I. I scrambled quickly to my feet. Then I got into my karate stance. It was the only thing I could think of.

But Buddy Gibson wasn't getting up. He lay on the floor, thrashing as if he were fighting an invisible enemy. His figure dimmed. Flickered—like a light-bulb that was about to burn out.

Whatever was happening, now was my chance to talk to him. I had to make him understand!

I wiped my face. I was sweating from fear.

"Listen, Gibson," I babbled. "You've got to believe me. I didn't do this on purpose. Someone . . . some*thing* did it to me. I don't know how it happened. I don't want to be here at all. Really!"

Gibson crawled away from me. He raised himself shakily against the wall. He was so dim now that I could barely see him.

"Not strong enough yet," Gibson whispered. "Next time. Next time I'll be stronger. I'll teach you to steal my life from me."

"But—"

Too late. Gibson disappeared.

And I was left standing there in his stupid cowboy pajamas.

I climbed back in bed, pulled the sheet up to my chin, and lay there, shivering. I was wide awake. No way I was going to close my eyes.

I could never stand up to another attack like that. Not if Gibson would be even stronger next time. I *had* to win that game tomorrow.

Before Gibson came back—and finished me off!

19

We boarded the bus the next day for our trip to the big game. The guys were all in high spirits. They clapped each other on the back and said things like "Reety-do!"

Reety-do?

I didn't think I would *ever* get used to this time.

I held my hand up for a high five, but all I got was a blank stare from Johnny Beans.

I took a seat beside Boog. He spent most of the ride bragging about how we were going to clobber the other team.

"We'll murderize them!" he announced. "Right, Buddy?"

"Uh—right," I agreed with a weak grin.

All I could think about was how hard I had to play.

Was it really possible for one guy to make the difference in winning and losing?

What if I couldn't do it?

While the other kids told jokes and laughed, I thought about how this was probably the next to last bus ride for all of us.

It was really depressing.

Finally we arrived. We tumbled off the bus. A big crowd had gathered for the game. The ballpark felt like a county fair. The air was filled with the good smells of hot dogs and hamburgers. Some guy was wandering around selling cotton candy.

We had a little batting practice. Boog slammed one pitch after the other over the fence. He was dead-on! Watching him, I started to feel a little more hopeful. If we all played like him, we might have a chance to turn things around!

I scanned the crowded bleachers. My eye stopped on Ernie, the bus driver. He sat in the top row. A big grin was plastered across his face.

"Be careful what you wish for," I muttered. "You just might get it."

Finally it was time to start. Our two teams lined up on opposite sides of the field while a high school band screeched through what was supposed to be *The Star-Spangled Banner*. The way they played it, it sounded more like a bunch of yowling cats.

After the song, one of the umpires flipped a coin. We won the toss. That meant we were the home team.

And we were up second. The coaches handed in their lineups to the plate umpire and shook hands.

The umpire raised his hand in the air. "Play ball!"

I sucked in a deep breath.

This was it!

By the fifth inning, the score was four to three. We were losing. And I was starting to get really scared.

I kept blowing easy plays. Like when one of the Wildcat batters popped a high one right to me.

"I got it!" I yelled. I danced back and forth as the ball came down. It was an easy out. Until the ball hit the edge of my glove and bounced over the foul line.

My whole team groaned.

"Hold it like a basket, Gibson!" Boog roared at me.

I ran after the ball. My face felt as if it were on fire.

I knew how the game was supposed to end. But I was starting to wonder. What if things didn't go the way they were supposed to? I mean, history was already different—because I wasn't really Buddy Gibson. I was in his body, sure, but how did I know how he would have played the game?

Maybe I had already messed up so badly that there was no way we could win.

Maybe I blew my chance to change history—and get back home.

No! I couldn't think that way!

The Wildcats had a second baseman who was just *amazing* at the plate. He was a skinny, short kid with glasses. But boy, could he swing a bat! No matter what he did, he couldn't help but get a hit.

By the seventh inning, the score was five to three. The Wildcats had two outs and runners on second and third. When the second baseman stepped in the batter's box, I groaned.

I was beginning to seriously hate that kid.

For the next few minutes, Wade, our pitcher, kept hurling strikes right over the inside corner of the plate. But the Wildcat batter kept fouling them off. Wade must have thrown him ten pitches, and the count was still no balls and two strikes.

At last Coach Johnson came trotting out to the mound. We all moved in.

"Walk him," Coach ordered.

"Oh, come on, Coach. I know I can get this guy," Wade protested.

Coach shook his head. "It's not worth it. He's too good. If he gets a hit, it'll be a homer—and then the Wildcats will score three runs. Walk him."

Suddenly I remembered something I'd seen once in a pro game.

"Hey, Coach. I have an idea," I whispered. Quickly I told him my plan.

Coach's eyes flashed. "I like it," he said quietly. He glanced at the catcher, then the pitcher. "Billy? Wade? You're the ones who have to make this work. Do you think you can do it?"

Billy and Wade nodded eagerly.

"Are we going to play ball here?" the umpire yelled.

Coach clapped his hands. "Okay, you heard me," he called loudly. But I saw him wink at Billy and Wade.

I took my base and watched Billy tug his mask back on. He stood behind the plate and held his right hand out wide.

"Are you guys going to chicken out and walk me?" the batter sneered.

"Wait and see," I answered under my breath.

Wade calmly threw the ball way wide of the plate.

"Ball one!" the umpire yelled.

Billy tossed it back.

Calls of "Chicken!" and *"Braawk!"* came from the Wildcats' dugout. Wade ignored them. He threw another way wide and Billy sent it back. Then again. The umpire called ball three.

Now was the time.

"Pay attention, ump," I muttered under my breath.

Billy still held his arm out wide. The batter glanced back at his jeering teammates and laughed. Wade threw again.

But instead of a wide one, he threw a fastball straight down the middle of the plate!

Billy squatted to catch it. The batter never even started his swing. His mouth fell open as the umpire yelled, "Stee-rike three! You're out!"

"Hey, no fair!" the batter yelled. "They can't do that."

Billy tossed the ball to the umpire. "We just did it, Einstein," he retorted. "Side retired."

Whooping with glee, we raced to the dugout. Coach stood grinning. "That was terrific, boys!"

I threw my glove on the bench. I felt much better, even though we were still behind two runs. There was a lot of game left. Plenty of time to make it up.

"Buddy," the coach called. "You're last at bat. Run out to the bus for me, would you? I left a pack of cigarettes on the front seat. Get them for me."

"Sure, Coach," I agreed.

I really should throw them away, I thought. But he would just buy more.

I ran out to the bus quickly. I didn't want to miss the game. As I got there, the doors folded open.

The bus driver must be in there, I thought.

But when I jumped up the steps, I was brought up short by the sight in the driver's seat.

Buddy Gibson!

There he was, right in broad daylight. Waiting for me. He looked strong. Solid. Not like a negative anymore.

"Oh, no!" I gasped.

He grinned.

"Oh, yes," he rasped. "And I'm not going away this time. *You* are!"

20

"**W**ait!" I cried. "You've got to listen to—"

That was all I got out. Then Gibson threw himself at me.

I fell backward. The air whooshed out of my lungs when I hit the ground. Gibson jumped down and sat on my chest. I struggled like crazy, trying to throw him off. But he was too strong.

"I'll teach you, you jerk," he panted. "I'll show you what it's like to be kicked out of your own body!"

He put his hands on my head. I felt the horrible wave of coldness again.

Then his fingers slid into my flesh.

They actually dipped into my skull!

"Noooo!" I yelled.

Icy fingers probed at my brain. Numbness stole over me. The world started to go dark.

This is it! I thought. I've had it!

Then I guess Buddy Gibson and I . . . merged.

It was the weirdest thing I ever experienced. All at once, I felt—bigger. Stronger. Faster.

I flexed my fingers. My hands felt as if I'd just taken off a pair of thick gloves.

For the first time, I really fit into Gibson's body.

I lay there on my back, breathing deeply. Energy pulsed through me.

Suddenly I felt a jolt of panic. Somehow I knew it wasn't coming from me.

"You're really from the future?" Gibson's voice gasped. *"And we're really going to be in a bus crash this afternoon?"*

His voice echoed off the inside of my skull. It wasn't a very comfortable feeling.

But at least I finally got someone to believe me!

"That's right. We all die—unless we win this game," I told him. I spoke out loud. It just seemed like the thing to do.

He didn't say anything. I couldn't tell whether he was even still in there.

"Gibson? Are you still there?" I asked.

There was no answer.

I climbed cautiously to my feet and brushed myself off.

From the distance I heard Boog shout, "Get a move on, Buddy!"

The game! I grabbed the coach's cigarettes and ran.

Maybe Gibson believed me. Maybe he didn't—and he was going to try to get me again.

But I couldn't worry about him now.

I still had a game to win!

21

I raced back to the ball field. "What's up?" I asked Johnny Beans.

"We got our third out already," he told me, shaking his head. "This game isn't going so well."

I grabbed my glove and hustled out to third base. I felt nervous. Antsy. I stalked around my base. "Come on, hit it my way," I muttered.

What was going on? I didn't usually feel like this.

"Wake up, man!" a voice snapped in my head. *"We've got to win this game!"*

"Gibson!" I exclaimed.

"No, it's the tooth fairy. Of course it's me! What, did you think I was going to skip the big game?"

He was still with me! Right there in my head!

At least he wasn't attacking me.

Not yet anyway.

"Heads up!" Gibson yelled. I jumped and glanced around wildly.

The ball whizzed past, near second base. A line drive. Straight to the hole in our outfield. This was bad. The Wildcats could get a triple.

Then I saw Boog. He raced across the field as if his shoes were on fire. He dove—and scooped the ball with his glove just before it hit the ground.

"Do it, Boog!" I yelled. What a play!

For the rest of the inning, Gibson kept quiet. I didn't know whether he was there inside me or not. But I didn't have much time to worry about it. I had to concentrate on the game!

At the top of the ninth, the score was five to three. We had two outs, and runners on first and second. I was on deck.

Then Billy Fein singled. Bases were loaded, and I was up.

As I stepped to home plate, I felt a surge of determination. I swung the bat and stared out at the pitcher.

I knew, I *knew* I was going to nail it.

That was Gibson inside me, I realized suddenly. He had a kind of confidence I'd never felt before. But I could feel it now.

He was working with me! Helping me!

The pitcher came at me with a hanging curveball. I grinned and clobbered that sucker.

I didn't even bother to watch it. I just tossed the bat aside and trotted the bases.

"Grand slam homer!" Boog roared from the dugout. "Gib-son! Gib-son!"

The batter after me struck out. Our side was retired. "So what?" Boog remarked as we trotted out to the field. "We're two runs up. The trophy is ours!"

But I knew differently. I remembered Ernie telling me how Shadyside led by two in the bottom of the ninth.

Just the way it was now.

History was repeating itself!

"Don't start celebrating yet," I cautioned.

"Win. We have to win!" said the voice in my head.

Gibson was so determined. It was like a fire inside me. I felt powerful. Alive.

But would it be enough? Would it change history?

And would that save the team and get me home?

22

The bottom of the ninth didn't start out well. Wade was tired, I guess. Anyway, the first Wildcat batter— that skinny second baseman with the glasses—hit a triple on the first pitch.

I winced. Not good. Definitely not good.

The next batter singled. So did the one after that. But at least I was able to keep the runner at third from going home.

The bases were loaded. Just the way Ernie described it.

The next batter stepped up. He hefted the bat with his left hand.

My stomach did a flip. "This is it," I said. "This is where it all happens!"

"Shut up and look sharp," Gibson warned in my head.

I was too scared to get annoyed.

I hugged the third baseline, but the rest of the team shifted over toward right field. "Move it, Buddy!" Coach Johnson yelled.

I ignored him.

"Buddy!" he yelled again.

I waved at him, but I didn't budge.

Coach called time and ran over to me.

"What do you think you're doing?" he demanded.

Oh, boy.

"I'm playing third," I replied, trying to sound innocent.

"I see. Are you playing third on my team?"

I gulped. "Uh—yes, sir."

"So why don't you move where I tell you to move?" he barked.

"He's going to push the ball to the left, Coach. I just know it," I argued.

"Oh, you know it, do you?" Coach snapped. "How do you know? Do you have a crystal ball or something?"

"Kind of," I mumbled.

"Oh, for Pete's sake." Coach sounded disgusted. "If you're not moving toward right in three seconds, I'll take you out of the game!"

I groaned, but I moved. What else could I do? I

stood there halfway to second, gazing tensely at that third base line.

The runners took their leads. The guy on second took such a big jump, he ended up only a few feet away from me.

The second the pitcher threw, I sprinted to the right.

WHAP! The batter cracked a line drive straight down the baseline.

"Go!" Gibson yelled in my head.

The ball screamed through the air. I'd never reach it! I'd never make it.

But then something swelled inside me. It couldn't get by. It *wouldn't* get by!

I leapt through the air. My arm stretched out so far, I thought my shoulder was going to pop.

"I got it!" I screamed.

The ball hit the tip of my glove.

And stuck. I squeezed my fingers around it.

One out!

It had seemed such a sure base hit, the runner was already halfway home. He turned and tore back toward third. From the ground, I reached out and slapped the base with my glove.

Double play. Two out!

Feet skidded behind me. Still flat on the ground, I rolled back toward second. The runner from second spun to go back. I rolled twice in the dirt and tagged the heel of his shoe.

Three out!

A triple play!

The game was over. And we won!

The crowd in the bleachers erupted in a huge roar. I lay there, staring up at the sky.

"Yes!" I screamed. "Yes!"

My teammates raced to me from all directions. They pulled me to my feet and then hoisted me onto their shoulders. We paraded around the field as the crowd cheered.

Boog was jumping up and down like an idiot. "An unassisted triple play! Did you see that?" he yelled to the whole world.

I was still dazed from what I did. What *we* did. Buddy Gibson and I. An unassisted triple play!

I went through the trophy ceremony in a daze of happiness and relief. In fact, it wasn't until I was on my second burger at the barbecue that it hit me.

Hold on a second!

"What am I still doing here?" I gasped.

"What's wrong?" Gibson asked inside my head.

"I'm still here," I muttered. "That's what's wrong! On TV the time traveler gets to leave after he does what he's supposed to do. What's the deal?"

Boog, who was standing nearby, turned and stared at me.

"Are you talking to me?" he asked.

"Uh—no," I said quickly. "I just said, 'What a meal!' There's so much to eat!"

"Yeah. Isn't it great?" Boog laughed and stuffed half a hot dog into his mouth.

"Maybe this doesn't work like TB," Gibson suggested.

"TV," I said under my breath.

"Whatever. What I'm saying is, maybe you can't go home." Gibson's voice was unusually quiet, for him. *"Maybe you're stuck here. With me."*

"You think?" My heart sank. "No. It can't be. There must be some delay or something. That's all."

"I hope so," he said. *"But just in case—are you any good at schoolwork?"*

I had to laugh.

Boog gave me a strange look. "What's so funny?" he asked.

"Oh, nothing," I answered.

"Come on, boys. Loading up," Coach Johnson called.

We all climbed on the bus. Soon it was whizzing down the road and we were on our way home. Everybody but me.

I closed my eyes. Maybe I even drifted off. Because I don't remember how long we'd been on the bus when it stalled.

Hrrrn, hrrnn, hrrrrrnnn, the starter moaned.

I sat up, bleary-eyed. "What is it?" I asked Boog.

"The bus is stalled," he answered.

The noise of the starter continued. "Don't flood it," Coach Johnson advised.

I peered sleepily out the window. Then I stared in horror.

A double thread of track ran below the bus and curved sharply to the right.

We were stalled on the railroad tracks!

My plan—it didn't work! We were all going to die anyway!

"We have to get out!" I yelled. *"Now!"*

"Simmer down, son," Ernie called. "It'll start in a minute."

"No. The train. The train!" I wailed. "It's going to hit us. Why won't you—" I broke off. Listening.

Oh, no. *No!*

The train's rumble came right through the floor of the bus.

"The train! It's coming!" Johnny Beans screeched.

"Oh, no!" Coach shouted. "Ernie, get us out of here!"

The starter whined. I could see the light from the train now.

"Let us out!" someone screamed.

But there was no time. The train barreled around the curve. Its light blared in my face.

We were done for!

23

"No!" I yelled.

It couldn't be! Not after I'd been through so much!

HRRRN! HRRRRN! The engine whined. The train roared closer. Its whistle shrieked.

Then the engine caught. The bus lurched and surged forward.

WHAM! Metal crunched as the train clipped the rear corner of the bus. We shot forward as if the bus were a rocket.

Ernie struggled with the wheel. The bus careened crazily back and forth across the road.

"Hold on, everybody!" he bellowed.

We were all yelling and screaming now. The smell of burning rubber filled my nose. I clutched the metal bar across the top of the seat desperately.

Then the bus ran off the road. I lost my grip and went flying. My head crashed against the window.

And that's the last thing I remember.

"Buddy? Buddy? Are you okay?"

I opened my eyes and saw the coach—*my* coach, Mr. Burress—looking down at me. I glimpsed Eve's face over his shoulder. Her mouth hung open so wide, you could have fit a baseball in there.

"All right!" I whispered.

I was back!

Coach Burress helped me to my feet.

"Send in Charlotte to pinch-run," he called over his shoulder.

"I'm okay. I'll shake it off," I protested.

"Shake it off? You just got clobbered in the head with a fastball. You're out of this game," Coach declared firmly.

Coach and Eve led me to the dugout. On the way, I gazed around, drinking in the sights. Red and blue uniforms that didn't look like sacks. Women in jeans instead of dresses. Normal cars.

I was really back!

"So—what did I miss?" I asked Eve, trying to sound casual.

"Miss?" Eve frowned. "You were knocked out for only about fifteen seconds. You didn't miss anything."

We reached the dugout. Both my mom and dad were there already, hovering. Mom dipped a cloth in the ice chest and held it to the place where the ball had got me.

"Mom, I'm all right, really," I told her.

She smoothed my hair back and gave me a worried look. "Are you sure, Buddy?"

"Yeah." I grinned. "I have a hard head."

Then I did something really embarrassing. I threw my arms around my mom and dad and hugged them both. Hard.

"My goodness!" Mom sounded surprised. "Thank you, sweetie! What brought that on?"

I flushed. "I don't know," I mumbled. "I just felt like it."

Mom glanced at Dad and raised her eyebrows. "Maybe we'd better take him to the doctor after all."

After I talked them out of that, I sat on the bench and watched Oneiga clobber us. Same old lousy Shadyside team.

Boy, was I glad to see them!

By the time we left the ball field though, I was starting to wonder. Everything here was so real. So normal. And even though I spent three days in 1948, it seemed that no time passed at all in the present.

Did I really travel in time?

Or did I just imagine it all?

Maybe the whole adventure happened in my mind!

I puzzled over it as Dad drove us toward Shadyside.

Eve was riding with us—her parents couldn't make it to the game.

We stopped off at the 7-Eleven on Village Road. Dad ran in for sodas. When he came back to the car, he tossed a couple of packs of baseball cards onto the backseat.

"Maybe that'll help make up for losing the game," he said.

I smiled. "Thanks, Dad."

"Yeah, thanks, Mr. Sanders," Eve echoed.

I picked up one of the packets and tore off the plastic wrapper. Eve leaned over to watch. "Get anything good?"

My mouth dropped in shock as I spotted the top card. It was a special issue on shiny, stiff paper with a gold border. A special Hall of Famer card.

Staring out at me was Buddy Gibson!

He looked older, of course. But it was definitely him. No way could I make a mistake about that. The caption said he played third base for the Yankees in the sixties.

"Oh, man!" Eve exclaimed. "A Buddy Gibson! You're so lucky. Those things are pretty rare."

I studied the card with a pounding heart.

So it wasn't a dream at all!

I *did* go back in time. I *did* change the past. No one died in that bus crash. And Buddy Gibson went on to the major leagues. To the Hall of Fame!

"Buddy Gibson." Eve sighed. "The most famous person who ever came from Shadyside. I sure would like to meet him. But he probably wouldn't have any time for a couple of kids."

I grinned. "I have a feeling he'd find time for us."

Because, thanks to me, Buddy Gibson had all the time in the world!

About R.L. Stine

R.L. Stine is the best-selling author in America. He has written more than one hundred scary books for young people, all of them bestsellers.

His series include *Fear Street, Ghosts of Fear Street* and the *Fear Street Sagas*.

Bob grew up in Columbus, Ohio. Today he lives in New York City with his wife, Jane, his teenage son, Matt, and his dog, Nadine.

Is The Roller Coaster Really Haunted?

THE BEAST

❑ 88055-1/$3.99

It Was An Awsome Ride—Through Time!

THE BEAST 2

❑ 52951-X/$3.99

A MINSTREL BOOK

Published by Pocket Books